SAVAGES

SAVAGES

A Nameless Detective Novel

Bill Pronzini

A Tom Doherty Associates Book
New York

SAVAGES: A NAMELESS DETECTIVE NOVEL

Copyright © 2007 by the Pronzini-Muller Family Trust

This book is printed on acid-free paper.

A Forge Book
Published by Tom Doherty Associates, LLC
175 Fifth Avenue
New York, NY 10010

www.tor-forge.com

Forge® is a registered trademark of Tom Doherty Associates, LLC.

ISBN-13: 978-0-7653-0933-4
ISBN-10: 0-7653-0933-5

First Edition: July 2007

Printed in the United States of America

0 9 8 7 6 5 4 3 2 1

For Melissa Meith and Mike White,
friends and neighbors,
with thanks for sharing a vital personal experience

SAVAGES

1

On Friday morning, I took Kerry to the U.C. Med Center for her first follow-up appointment with her radiologist and her oncologist.

As I had during the long weeks of radiation therapy, I waited for her in the lobby. When she came out, as she had all the other times, she wore a small, determined smile. "So far so good," she said.

"What did they say?"

"Come back in one month. Meanwhile go home, talk about cancer in the past tense, and live my life."

"Is that supposed to be encouraging?"

"Actually, yes. As good as it gets at this point."

On the drive home to Diamond Heights, as on previous drives, we engaged in bright, upbeat conversation. Her spirits were always good in my presence, and I made sure that mine were in hers. It was vital that we maintain a positive outlook. Any doctor will tell you that mental attitude is important in the treatment of any disease, particularly one as life threatening as breast cancer.

In the beginning it hadn't been easy for us to remain upbeat, even though the odds were in our favor. Breast cancer is no longer an automatic death sentence for a woman; the survival rate is high when the malignancy is found and treated early. Still, the first couple of months are a pretty tense time. First we'd had to wait for the results of the DNA test to determine whether her father was Ivan Wade, as she'd always believed, or her mother's writer acquaintance and rapist, Russell Dancer. If it were Dancer, the situation would have been even more difficult, because he was dead now and had been an orphan and kept no personal records; tracing his family medical history would've been next to impossible. But the DNA test turned out right, thank God. Kerry was Ivan's child.

That was the first piece of good news. The second was that the tumor in her right breast proved to be relatively small and the cancer hadn't become invasive; her oncologist, Dr. Janek, had recommended and performed a lumpectomy rather than a more radical type of surgery. Three weeks of healing time were followed by five weeks of radiation therapy—thirty-three treatments altogether, the first twenty-five focusing on the entire breast area, the remaining eight on the much smaller surgery site. The treatments made Kerry tired, listless much of the time. She hated the necessary tattooing of her skin—little blue dots so that the radiation machine could be placed in exactly the same location each time for maximum effect—and she developed a healthy dislike for her radiologist for what she called his "dehumanizing treatment" of his patients. But her body chemistry was such that she didn't suffer the worst side effect, severe burning of the radiated areas that results in a painful condition the doctors call "skin breakup." As it was, the cumulative effects produced some skin reddening and cracks toward the end of the schedule, made her skin feel stiff and rigid like cardboard. She insisted the soreness and discomfort were tolerable, but it hurt me every time I saw this outward abuse of her body—a constant reminder that the cure could sometimes be as savage as the illness.

More cause for optimism at the end of the six-week period. The radiation bombardment seemed to have had the desired effect of killing any remaining infected cells. Dr. Janek was not recommending any other treatment at this point, no drugs that might cause weight gain and night sweats and be a constant reminder to Kerry that she was still an at-risk cancer patient.

When the radiation therapy first started, Kerry had slept a lot, spent her waking hours in bed or propped up on the couch in the living room, reading, watching TV. Gradually, as her body adjusted, she was able to function more or less normally for short periods, do little things around the condo, take short outings. And she'd made arrangements with Bates and Carpenter to handle a limited amount of work from home. Her energy level now was such that she felt she would be ready to go back to work full-time in ten days. I thought that was a little premature, but if Dr. Janek gave his permission I wouldn't try to talk her out of it.

Long, hard two-plus months. For me, for Cybil, Kerry's mother, who was eighty-three and in shaky health herself, and for Emily. When we first told the kid, she'd had some trouble coming to terms with it; she had suffered so much loss already in her young life, the sudden deaths of both her natural parents, and the prospect of losing her adoptive mother as well was devastating. If the breast cancer diagnosis had come two years ago, Emily might not have been emotionally equipped to weather it, as fragile as she'd been when she first came to live with us, but she was stronger now, more mature, more secure. Once the initial shock passed she'd shown the kind of strength and courage we'd hoped for.

As for me, I'd all but quit working during July and August, so I could be with Kerry at the hospital every day and take care of Emily and the household chores and bring Cybil over from Larkspur for periodic visits, since she was no longer able to drive long distances. I didn't get much sleep, had no appetite, and lost ten pounds. Tension and anger lived in me day and night. The first few times I saw Kerry pale and tired after radiation, then later that spreading burn on her chest, the frustration I felt was so great I wanted to hit something—a wall, a door, something. Because I loved her and I couldn't stand to see her like that. Because there was nothing I could to do to help her. All I could do was watch, wait, hope, pray, remain positive—passive roles that go against my nature.

There was anxiety, too, constant and insidious. Despite all the good news and reason for optimism, there were no guarantees that Kerry would continue to be a survivor. Cancer is a devious goddamn disease. You think you've got it beat, all the signs point in that direction, and then without warning it can flare up again in the same spot or in some other part of the body, and if it does, then maybe it *will* be invasive; maybe you *won't* survive. You can never be completely sure this won't happen. You can never feel completely safe.

We both knew that, but we never mentioned it. Once during the first week of radiation therapy I came home after running an errand, walked in quietly, and heard Kerry crying in the bedroom. Great, heart-wrenching sobs that tore through me like knives. She never wept when I was around, not so much as a single tear. I know that crying is a healthy thing for a woman, a form of cartharsis, but I don't seem able to cope with it; it turns me to jelly inside, unmans me. I slipped out even more quietly, wandered around the neighborhood for a while, and made a lot of noise when I let myself back into the condo. Kerry was dry-eyed and smiling in bed. Episode over and done with, as if it had never happened. But not forgotten, not ever, by me.

I hated those devious, unstable bastard cells in her body and what they had done to her emotionally as well as physically. A greater, more virulent hatred than I've ever felt for anything or anybody in my life.

• • •

Late that Friday morning, after I took Kerry home from the hospital, I drove downtown to the new agency offices on South Park. She didn't need me for anything, and Emily was off at Marine World with a friend and the friend's parents, and it was time I put in an appearance. What with one thing and another, I hadn't been in all week.

Tamara was on the phone when I walked in, and the new part-time hire, Alex Chavez, was getting ready to leave. Jake Runyon figured to be out in the field somewhere, as per usual. Everything running smoothly, also as per usual.

Chavez said an effusive "good morning" and immediately asked after Kerry. The question, unlike the greeting, was delivered with what seemed to be genuine concern and a sober countenance. Usually Alex was all smiles and good cheer—one of those rare breeds, a genuinely happy man. He was from El Centro, in the Imperial Valley, where he'd been a deputy sheriff and then an investigator with the D.A.'s office. Late thirties, dark, wiry, married with four kids, religious in the true Christian way. Moved to the Bay Area two years ago at his wife's urging to be near her aging mother and father. When Tamara and I decided we could use another operative, because of the situation with Kerry and the agency's increasingly heavy caseload, we'd put out feelers and Chavez had been recommended to us by another of the city's investigative services who had employed him on a part-time basis. A thirty-minute interview coupled with his résumé was all we needed to hire him. He'd proven to be the right choice, just as Runyon had before him. Honest, efficient, uncomplaining, and so upbeat you couldn't spend five minutes in his company without some of it rubbing off on you.

I told him Kerry was doing well, and he nodded and smiled and said he and his wife were praying for her. A man I'd known less than three months, a part-time employee, and he was including the wife of one of his bosses, a woman he'd never met, in his prayers. I needed people like Alex Chavez in my life, now more than ever. People who took the edge off my general cynicism and helped to renew some of my faith in humanity.

"What're you working on, Alex?"

"Anderson case. Joseph Anderson, nonpayment of child support?"

"Right. Any leads on his whereabouts?"

"A couple. I'll find him sooner or later. If there's one breed I can't stand, it's deadbeat fathers."

"Same here."

"My old man was one," he said.

"Oh? Sorry to hear it."

"Not a problem anymore. I found him, years ago, over in Tucson. Made him pay up most of what he owed my mother. He didn't like the idea, but he didn't have any choice when I got through talking to him."

"Good for you."

"So guys like this Anderson are a piece of cake," Chavez said, and went out smiling.

In my office, I found three messages waiting for me. Out of the agency loop for nearly a full week, and all I had were three messages. And two of those were from professional acquaintances concerned about Kerry. The lack of business communications was a reminder—as if I needed another one—that I was no longer an essential part of the agency I'd founded and built up and nurtured for nearly thirty years. Hadn't been for some time. It was Tamara's now; she ran it with far more efficiency than I ever had, was making it grow and prosper. Runyon and now Chavez carried out most of the fieldwork I'd once handled almost entirely on my own. There wasn't much for me to do even at the best of times. Retirement is a concept I don't much like—I don't play golf, the only hobby I have, collecting old pulp magazines, doesn't take up much time, and I chafe under enforced inactivity—so I kept on working whenever I could, as much as I could. But except on infrequent occasions, it wasn't the same anymore. Everything changes, sure, and this was exactly why I disliked and resisted change.

The third message was clipped to a case-file folder. Tamara's scrawl read: *Call Celeste Ogden.* Followed by a phone number and the comment *Déjà vu all over again.*

The name Celeste Ogden meant nothing to me until I opened the folder. Then I remembered her, and not with any pleasure. One of my cases, some four years old. Routine stuff, or should have been. I was scanning through the report, refamiliarizing myself with the details, when

Tamara finished her call and came in through the connecting door.

I was struck again, as sometimes happened when I hadn't seen her for a week or more, by what a handsome, poised young woman she was—a far cry from the grunge-dressed, wiseass militant she'd been when she first came to work for me. A lot had happened in her life in those five years, personal and professional both, the combination of which had matured her, added character and patience and determination. She was still very much her own woman, but she had goals and direction now, where before she'd been something of a loose cannon. What she wanted now was for this agency to be successful enough to rival McCone Investigations and the other big outfits in the city, and by God she intended to have her way. I envied her. For her drive and her youth and her health and all the possibilities that lay in her future.

She said, leaning against the doorjamb, "Good news on Kerry's checkup or you wouldn't be here." Making it a statement rather than a question. She'd been a hundred percent supportive during the crisis; you couldn't have asked more of a friend and business partner.

"So far so good," I said.

"How you doing? Getting enough sleep?"

"Now I am. You don't need as much when you get to be my age."

"Right," she said. "Old Father Time."

"Sixty-two must seem ancient to you."

"Nope. Pop just turned sixty and he can still outrun me in the hundred-yard dash." She came closer, the better to give me a critical once-over. "Worry lines, not age lines," she said. "They get any deeper, you're gonna look like a map of the Mojave Desert."

"Yeah, well," I said.

"Not gonna change anything by worrying. But it'll change *you* in the long run."

"Tamara Corbin, philosopher. How's Tamara Corbin, young woman about town?"

"You asking about my love life?"

"Peripherally." She'd broken up with Horace, her long-time boyfriend, three months ago—or rather, he'd quit her, long-distance from Philadelphia, for another woman—and it had been rough on her for a while. "Just wondering how you're doing."

"I'm cool. My love life's ice-cold."

"Still haven't met anyone new?"

"Not looking. Just me and Mr. V, for now."

"Who's Mr. V?"

"My vibrator. We're going steady. Practically engaged."

I should know better by now than to ask an outspoken young person like Tamara personal questions; they produce more candid information than an old fart can comfortably process. I said, "Moving right along," and tapped the Celeste Ogden message slip attached to the file folder. "What's this all about?"

"Same as before—her sister and brother-in-law. That's all she'd say. She wants you, nobody else."

"When did she call?"

"Yesterday afternoon. Told her you might not be available until next week."

"Didn't put her off?"

"Not her. She got pushy, I pushed back, and she hung up on me. But then she called again a few minutes later, all stiff and formal, and tried to make nice. She even said *please* have you call her as soon as possible. I said I'd give you the message and hung up on her."

"The Tamara method of winning friends and influencing people."

"Most of 'em like it when I go that route. Detective's supposed to be tough, right? No-nonsense. Makes clients feel like they're getting their money's worth."

"Ex-client, in her case," I said. "I'm not interested in putting up with her obsession again."

"For a big fee, we can put up with anybody's obsession. That's our new agency motto—I just made it up."

"Then let Jake deal with her."

"She wants you. Besides, his plate's full. Hollowell skip-trace, a subpoena to deliver up near Red Bluff, and witness interviews and legwork for the defense team on a homicide case starting next week."

"What homicide case is that?"

"Parking garage shooting in North Beach six weeks ago. The defendant has enough bucks to afford Avery Young as his attorney. And Young handed the investigative job to us two days ago." Tamara's eyes shone. "We do a good job on this one, and we will, it won't be the last for his firm."

"Nice."

"That's what I'm talking about. Score!"

"What's Alex got other than the Anderson job?"

"Enough preliminary work on the Young case for two operatives. So Celeste Ogden is up to you."

"Lucky me."

Tamara's phone rang and she retreated into her office to answer it. I opened the file folder again, thinking: So now I'm the mop-up guy. Weirdos and recalcitrants, my speciality. Yeah, lucky me.

All right. Background investigation requested by Mrs. Celeste Ogden on one Brandon Mathias, who at the time, nearly four years ago, was engaged to marry her widowed older sister, Nancy Ring. Mrs. Ogden neither liked nor trusted Mathias; she considered him cold, ruthless, self-involved, pathologically ambitious, and several other unflattering things and was convinced he was marrying her sister for her money and the business Nancy Ring had inherited from her first husband. The business, RingTech, was a small but very profitable manufacturer of computer software for businesses, located in Palo Alto.

I'd done what I considered to be a thorough check on Mathias, all the way back to his youth in northern Ohio, and I hadn't found anything to support Celeste Ogden's suspicions. He came from a well-to-do family; he'd graduated with honors from both high school and Ohio University, the latter with a degree in computer science; he'd landed a position with a Silicon Valley firm during the boom years, made all the right contacts and all the right professional decisions, worked his way up to an executive position at an annual salary in excess of $200,000. No question that he was ambitious, maybe even to the point of ruthlessness, but so are a lot of men and women in this country. As far as his personal life went, there wasn't so much as a smudge: no previous marriages, no questionable relationships, no brushes with the law, not even a hint of unethical business practices.

I was satisfied, but Celeste Ogden wasn't. If anyone was pathological, it was her. She was convinced that Mathias was some sort of Hyde in Jekyll guise. She insisted I dig deeper, keep digging until I found something. I don't much like that kind of excavation; everybody has some unflattering secret buried in his past, and if it's small enough and irrelevant enough, it should be allowed to remain buried. But in my business you don't just blow off a client who has plenty of money—her husband was a well-regarded vascular surgeon—and no set time limit for results, even if you don't particularly like her.

So I dug and kept on digging, and I still didn't find anything. Brandon Mathias wasn't a saint, but neither was he much of a sinner. If he had any buried secrets, they were down so deep a team of detectives working round the clock couldn't locate them. Obsessive-compulsive in his drive for success was about the harshest criticism you could apply to him. Maybe that was why he was marrying Nancy Ring, but even if so, it wasn't a hanging offense. And he wouldn't be fooling her, either. She was forty-three years old and had been married to a Silicon Valley mover and shaker for nearly twenty years; she had to be going into the marriage with her eyes wide open.

I'd said all of this to Ogden, verbally and in my report, and in return I'd got a heaping of abuse. She was one of these moneyed types used to giving orders, having things her own way. She didn't like it when her opinions went unvalidated, and when that happened she blamed the other party, not herself. She claimed I hadn't done my job properly, hinted that I was incompetent—like that. I wouldn't take it from her. I don't take that kind of crap from anybody. As politely as I could under the circumstances, I defended my work ethic and the results of my investigation, suggested she take her suspicions to another agency, and terminated the relationship. I half-expected to have to take her to small-claims court to collect the balance of our fee, but she surprised me by paying the final invoice by return mail.

That was the last I'd heard from or about her. Whether or not she'd hired another investigator, she hadn't succeeded in stopping the wedding: the "brother-in-law" reference to Tamara proved that. Now after four years Ogden was back knocking on my door again, and not so imperiously this time. Why? I didn't want to work for her again, but I was curious enough to listen to what she had to say.

I dialed the number on the message slip. A woman with a Spanish accent answered, asked for my name, and went away to deliver it. Ten seconds later Celeste Ogden was on the line, thanking me for returning her call. The voice was familiar, low pitched and aggressive, but the inflection was different. Subdued, tinged with something I couldn't quite identify.

"I imagine you were surprised to hear from me again," she said, "after such a long time."

"Yes, I was."

"I didn't know who else to call. The police . . . they won't listen to me. I need someone to *listen* to me."

"Police, Mrs. Ogden?"

"They say it was an accident, that it couldn't be anything else. But they're wrong. I don't care what anyone says. He did it. He's responsible."

"Did what?"

"Nancy's dead," she said in a cold, flat voice. "My sister is dead and that bastard killed her."

2

Celeste Ogden lived on the upper westward slope of Nob Hill, in the penthouse of an ornate apartment house built in the twenties. I'd been there before, four years ago, so I knew what to expect. The liveried doorman gave me the kind of fish-eyed look his breed reserves for the lower variety of salesman until I dropped the Ogden name and said I was expected; then he shifted into mock deferential and allowed me to enter. A room-sized elevator whisked me up six floors about as fast as a race car accelerating from zero to sixty. The penthouse had a double-door entrance and chimes that rang with a cathedral-like resonance. A Latina maid, probably the same one who'd answered the phone, opened the door and silently conducted me into a massive sunroom, where she left me to wait.

The room, which opened onto a broad terrace strewn with stone statuary, reeked of old money and old-fashioned elegance. Heavy teak and mahogany furniture, Oriental carpets, Tiffany lamps, gilt-framed paintings of what looked to be old Dutch burghers and their families in various stages of a picnic. It should have been bright and cheerful, with golden afternoon sunlight streaming in through the floor-to-ceiling windows, but it wasn't. It had an aloof, museum-like aspect enhanced by a hushed silence.

I wandered over to an unused fireplace. On the mantel was a gilt-framed photograph of Celeste Ogden and a white-maned, white-mustached man some twenty years her senior. I'd never met her husband, but the gent in the photo had the distinguished, self-confident look of a successful vascular surgeon. He also had a possessive hand placed firmly on her shoulder. I moved from there to the windows. Hundred-and-eighty-degree view: cityscape, the Bay, Alcatraz and Angel Islands, the Golden Gate Bridge. Add a few thousand a month, minimum, to whatever exorbitant rent the Ogdens were paying. If they were renting; for all I knew, they owned this penthouse.

I'd been there about a minute and a half when Celeste Ogden came in. In one hand she carried a white, shirt-sized gift box. She apologized for keeping me waiting, thanked me again for agreeing to see her. Subdued, all right, but that didn't affect the imperious, iron-willed air she projected. Or the simmering anger that was evident in her gray eyes. She was past forty now, but she didn't look it. Slim, trim, her sharp-chinned face unlined and glowing in a way that indicated a recent face-lift; dark hair perfectly coiffed, beige pantsuit that appeared to be silk and was as unwrinkled as her skin, a gold locket at her throat, and rings galore.

The diamond wedding rock on her left hand threw off daggers of reflected sunlight as sharp as laser beams.

She invited me to sit down, sat herself on a round-backed couch with tufted velvet upholstery, and laid the box down beside her. I perched on the edge of a matching chair with my hands flat on my knees. I could feel sweat under the collar of my shirt. Surroundings like this, women like her, always made me feel poorly dressed, poorly socialized, and vaguely inadequate. Kerry says it's low self-esteem and there's no good reason for it. She's right about the low self-esteem, anyway.

I said, "As I said on the phone, Mrs. Ogden, I doubt there's anything I can do for you."

"Reserve judgment, please, until you've heard what I have to say."

Whatever that was, she'd insisted on saying it in person rather than over the phone. And offered to pay me for my time if I'd come see her, whether I agreed to help her or not. That was as much the reason I was here as curiosity about the circumstances of her sister's sudden death.

"And try to keep an open mind," she added. "You may think me an unduly fixated and suspicious woman, based on our past association, but I assure you I'm not. I have good reason for my feelings about my brother-in-law."

"Suppose you start by telling me how your sister died."

"It was prominent in the media. You didn't see any of the news stories?"

"I'm sorry, no, I didn't." That was because I make it a policy not to read newspapers or watch TV reportage.

There are news junkies and then there's me, the anti–news junkie.

Celeste Ogden drew a deep breath, composing herself, before she said, "The official verdict was an accidental fall. Down a long staircase at her home in Palo Alto . . . severe head trauma. It happened sometime between ten and eleven at night and the light in the upstairs hall was burned out. The police believe she was on her way downstairs for some reason and tripped in the darkness."

"But you don't think it was an accident."

"No, I don't. She was pushed or thrown down those stairs."

"By her husband?"

"By his order. He's much too calculating to have done it himself. He was in Chicago when it happened, at a business conference." Ridges of anger puckered her mouth, bent it down tight at the corners. "The perfect arranged alibi, while somebody else did his dirty work."

Hired killing? Well, maybe. It isn't as easy to hire a hit man as Hollywood and fiction writers would have you believe, particularly for corporate businessmen like Brandon Mathias who move in the upper echelons of society. On the other hand, if you're cunning and ballsy enough and you've got enough money to spread around, anything is possible.

I asked, "Your sister was alone in the house at the time?"

"Except for whoever killed her, yes."

"No evidence of an intruder?"

"None. Nothing was disturbed and all the doors and

windows were locked. The only way anyone could have gotten in was with a key, and he is the only person who could have provided one."

Not quite true. Keys can be lost and found, or obtained in other ways. Nancy Mathias could also have let another person into the house, someone she knew or a fast-talking stranger with the right kind of story. But there was no benefit in pursuing any of that now.

"Who found the body?" I asked.

"Her cleaning woman, early the following morning. Philomena worked for Nancy for several years and had a key to the house."

So much for providing that angle. "You said you had good reason to suspect your brother-in-law, Mrs. Ogden. What would that be, exactly?"

She arranged her hands in her lap, palms up, one on top of the other, and sat staring at them for a few seconds before she said, "Have you ever lost someone close to you, someone you loved very much?"

Uh-uh, I thought, I'm not going there. Not with her, not with anybody at this point in my life. "No," I said. And I'm not going to.

"It's devastating. Totally devastating. Nancy and I were very close, or at least we were until the past couple of years. She was my only sibling, the only person I cared deeply about other than my husband. When you have that sort of connection, your life becomes intertwined with the other person's. You develop a sixth sense where they're concerned that allows you to intuit things about them and the people close to them. By observation and . . . osmosis, if you will. You understand?"

"Very well, yes."

"There was a great deal wrong in my sister's life since her marriage, especially during the past few months, and all of it was directly related to *him*." Slight inflection on the pronoun. "He" and "him" every time she referred to Mathias, as if she couldn't bear to speak his name.

"How do you mean 'wrong'?"

"She wasn't the same person after she married him. I sensed it would be that way—the reason I hired you to investigate him—and that was the way it was. Before she met him, she was high-spirited, vivacious . . . a word you don't hear much anymore, but it describes Nancy perfectly. Afterward she grew distant, withdrawn, secretive, almost reclusive—a shadow of her former self, living in his shadow. His doing. I told you before he was a controlling personality."

"Did he abuse her?"

"Not physically, so far as I know. Verbally, yes, oh yes. But never in public, of course. Cold, manipulative . . . a psychological abuser."

"His wife as a possession, molded to his will?"

"Exactly. Everyone, including Nancy, is just an object to him. He has no compassion or other human feelings. All he understands is his own ambition."

"And she tolerated this?"

"Nancy was . . . malleable. And needy, very needy."

"Did she ever talk to you about her relationship with her husband?"

"Not to me, nor to anyone else. She was devoted to him; he could do no wrong in her eyes until recently. She defended him so fiercely whenever I brought up an issue that it was impossible to get through to her."

"Until recently, you said. She showed signs of rebellion toward the end?"

"Not rebellion, exactly, no. The last time I saw her was four months ago, and then only for a few minutes. She wouldn't return my phone calls or answer my e-mails."

"If his control over her was that complete," I said carefully, "why would he want her dead?"

"That is what I want you to find out."

"Another woman?"

"I suppose that's possible, although so far as I know he has never shown any interest in other women."

"Bad investments? Illegal transactions of some kind?"

"Either one is possible," she said. "I wouldn't put anything past him."

"I take it there was no prenuptial agreement?"

"I begged Nancy to have one drawn, but she wouldn't hear of it. She believed that marriage is based on trust. If you couldn't trust a man, you had no business marrying him in the first place."

"So he inherits everything."

"Yes. The company, her bank accounts, everything."

"Approximately how much does the estate amount to?"

"In liquid assests, more than three million dollars."

Plenty of motive for murder. But again, why would Mathias take the risk if he had her bent to his will? There'd have to be some other compelling reason besides financial gain. I asked, "Do you have any evidence, anything other than intuition, that Mathias was responsible for your sister's death?"

"If I did, I would have taken it to the police and he'd be in jail now where he belongs." She paused, her eyes narrowing. "Are you one of these men who scoff at women's intuition?"

"Not at all. I don't doubt that you believe she was murdered and your brother-in-law arranged it."

"But that's not enough for you."

"I didn't say that. You know the people involved; I don't. Does your husband feel as you do?"

"My husband?" She looked at me as if I'd made an offensive remark. "Why would you ask that?"

"No particular reason. It was just a question."

"Dr. Ogden is a very busy man," she said stiffly, as if that were an appropriate answer. Maybe it was. "I have his complete trust and support."

"I'm sure you do."

"I don't expect the same from you," she said, "but I'd like you . . . no, I *need* you to give me the benefit of the doubt. As much as I wish I were capable of proving his guilt myself, I simply don't have the knowledge or the skills. You do."

"There are other detective agencies—"

"But you already have a dossier on him and an understanding of my position. I trust you and I have faith in the thoroughness of your methods."

"You weren't so sure about that four years ago."

"Four years ago," she said, "I was a different person than I am now. Four years ago my sister was still alive."

Awkward moment. I managed not to squirm. She was practiced at getting her way, and this whole conversation had been carefully manipulated with alternating prods of pathos, praise, and subtle demand. Even so, I couldn't blame her. Her hatred of her brother-in-law may have been misguided, but both her grief and her conviction were genuine.

Saying no to someone in distress has never been easy for me. I tried to say it now, and what came out instead was a hedge: "I can't conduct the sort of investigation you're asking for on the basis of intuition alone. I've already done a deep background check on the man without turning up anything. If he's as cunning as you say, there won't be anything to find in the past four years, either. And if he is guilty of murder, he'll have covered himself twice as thoroughly. Without some concrete facts as a starting point, I just don't think I could—"

"What sort of facts?"

"Unusual recent occurrences in his life or hers. Anything out of the norm that might support the assumption of violence. Letters, messages, unexplained bills, that sort of thing."

"A diary?"

"Or a diary, yes."

She smiled faintly, a constrictive upward movement at the corners of her mouth, and picked up the white gift box and held it out to me.

"What's this?"

"Open it."

I took it from her. Inside were a dozen or so computer discs, each of which bore a set of dates, and several business-size envelopes and small manila envelopes stuffed with papers. I looked into a few of them: insurance policies, itemized credit card bills, utility and property tax bills, check registers and canceled checks, miscellaneous items that couldn't be identified at a glance.

"Nancy's," she said. "All of it."

"Where did you get it?"

"From her study at her home. The day after she died, before he came back from Chicago."

"You have a key to the house?"

"No. He wouldn't allow it. I went to see Philomena and convinced her to let me have hers."

"Does Mathias know you took all this?"

"I don't know. He didn't say anything about it at the funeral. Hardly spoke a word to me."

"What's on the computer discs?"

"Nancy kept a daybook. Faithfully, every day, since she was a child. Usually just a few lines about her day, impressions, and so on."

"Up to the time of her death?"

"To the very night, in fact."

"So you've read everything on the discs?"

"More than once. The rest, too, of course."

"And?"

"Hints, little things that I'm at a loss to explain—out of the norm, as you put it. You'll be able to tell what they are, I think."

"Suppose you tell me."

"I'd rather you discover them for yourself." The faint nonsmile again. "Without my biased input."

I said, "I didn't know your sister or anything about her private life."

"You'll know enough by the time you've examined everything in that box."

Probably more than I'd ever want to know, I thought.

"Just study it all with an open mind," Celeste Ogden said, "that's all I ask. When you're done, I think you'll understand why I don't believe Nancy's death was an accident."

"Maybe so. But I still may not want to undertake this sort of investigation—"

"Of course you will," she said in her imperious way. She got to her feet. "Excuse me a moment," and away she went, leaving me alone with my doubts and the box full of a dead woman's private leavings.

I pushed the contents around again with the tips of two fingers. But my mind wasn't on Nancy Mathias. It was Kerry I was thinking about when Celeste Ogden came back into the room. This time what she had in her hand was a check.

"One thousand dollars," she said. "That's sufficient for the time being, I trust."

I had the feeling, holding the check, that she hadn't just made it out; that it had been written long before I got there. A woman used to getting her own way, all right. A woman you couldn't say no to in a situation like this, no matter how hard you tried.

3

JAKE RUNYON

It started out as just another routine assignment.

Some operatives would consider it dull routine—deliver a subpoena to a reluctant witness in a robbery-assault case—but it was the kind he liked because it entailed a road trip. He felt better when he was on the move. Didn't matter where he went or why. Driving, moving, energized him, gave him a measure of peace that he seldom found when he was caught between four walls.

The road trip in this case would be manageable in one long day if the timing were right, but he had other agency business to take care of that Friday and he couldn't get out of the city until early afternoon. The subpoena could have waited until Monday for delivery, but he never felt right about putting off a job when he had the opportunity to do it immediately—the more so when there was a static weekend to be gotten through. As it was, he'd stay over in a motel somewhere around Gray's Landing. The four-hour run back to San Francisco would use up most of Saturday morning and he could stretch the day out with a detour or two.

This Saturday was the first in weeks he hadn't been able to fill up with work. Busy summer, lots of overtime—also just the way he liked it. What he didn't like was the reason behind the heavy workload. He didn't know Bill or his wife very well, Kerry hardly at all, but the news of her breast cancer had slammed him a little because of Colleen. Ugly damn coincidence. He knew what they were going through, both of them. Breast tumor, surgery, radiation—that was bad, but at least it was the curable kind of cancer with a high survival rate. Ovarian cancer, the kind Colleen had had, was a death sentence. Six months of pain and fading hopes and not-so-quiet desperation before she was finally, mercifully gone. But it would never be over for him. He would continue to live with the suffering, hers and his both, every day and every night until he drew his last breath. He hoped to God, if there was a God, that Bill wouldn't have to do the same.

During those terrible months of watching Colleen die, Runyon had developed the ability to shut himself down inside without losing awareness—a kind of catlike patience that kept external forces beyond his control from touching him, kept the pain and the memories more or less at bay. He did that now, as he crept across the Bay Bridge. Friday traffic was already at a crawl, and pretty much stayed that way up Highway 80 and across the Carquinez Bridge. More than an hour before it cleared enough for him to run at the speed limit; it could have been ten hours and it wouldn't have affected him any differently.

He drove at a steady sixty-five up 80 to the 505 connector and then due north on Highway 5. Fifteen degrees hotter by the time he passed Willows, even though it was well after five o'clock by then. Late September heat, dry and dusty, shimmering on the asphalt and across the flat brown farm country that stretched all the way to Red Bluff.

Gray's Landing was some twelve miles south of Red Bluff. Agricultural area: olives, almonds, walnuts, peaches. Cattle and sheep ranching. That was all he knew about it. When he'd first moved down from Seattle two years ago, he'd spent a lot of time familiarizing himself with San Francisco and the other Bay Area cities, traveling some of the main arteries and back roads that threaded the rural areas of northern California. The theory being that the better a man knew the area he was working in, the better he could do his job. He'd been to Red Bluff and Redding and some of the other towns in Tehama and Glenn and Butte counties, but he'd missed Gray's Landing. You couldn't cover every bit of ground within a couple of thousand square miles. Eventually, maybe, but not in only two years.

He took the first exit, drove a half mile or so through orchards and a big new sprawl of a shopping center.

Turned into the first service station he saw for gas and information. He got the gas all right, but the big red-haired attendant couldn't tell him where Old Stage Road was. No surprise; the kid looked as if he might have to check his driver's license if somebody asked him his name. One stoplight beyond the station was a no-frills motel with an attached coffee shop. Runyon got everything he needed there. The clerk gave him a room key and easy-to-follow directions to Old Stage Road. He stayed in the room long enough to deposit his overnight bag, wash up, and change his shirt. Stayed in the coffee shop long enough to drink a sweaty glass of iced tea. Then he got back into the overheated Ford and followed the road through the center of Gray's Landing.

Small farm town, the kind that still exists in backwater sections of California—the kind that makes you think you've passed through a time warp and come out fifty years in the past. Old buildings, their age-worn surfaces softened by the mellow gold evening light—some of Spanish-style adobe brick, others of wood with false fronts, the tallest an art deco movie theater whose marquee proclaimed that it was now the home of the First Pentecostal Church of Gray's Landing. Several storefronts were empty, victims of the new shopping center and America's fixation with big-box consumerism. There wasn't much traffic at this time of evening; the streets and sidewalks had an air of desertion, like a backlot film set that was no longer used.

There'd been a big fire in the town recently. At the far

end of Main, beyond a heat-seared park with droopy shade trees and a central bandstand, he passed the blackened remains of a school. Big blaze that had gutted most of the buildings and left the entire block-square lot looking like a bombed-out battlefield.

Baseball and soccer fields, small complex of medical-dental offices, and then he was in open country again. After half a mile he came to an intersection; he turned right, drove another half mile, and when he turned right again he was on Old Stage Road. More orchards interspersed with hay fields and dry brown grassland, spotted with humps of bare rock and oak and madrone trees. Farm roads and farm buildings scattered here and there. Slat and barbed-wire fences. Cattle, sheep, horses, a couple of grazing donkeys. All of it bore the parched look of a hot, dry summer.

The sun was low on the horizon to the west, spilling the beginnings of a fiery sunset into the sky, when he found the place he was looking for. Black letters on a weathered sign above the entrance to a paved access road read: **Belsize Farm.** He turned in, followed the road through groves of walnut trees, over a rise, down into a long hollow. The farm buildings were spread out there, along the willow-shaded bank of a creek—farmhouse, large barn, smaller barn, two other outbuildings, chicken coop, vegetable garden. The scorch of summer lay over the farm, too; it all had the same wilted aspect as the stalks in the garden, the climbing roses along the house porch.

A dust-streaked pickup truck was parked in the farm-yard, the only vehicle other than a tractor in sight. Run-yon pulled up next to it, got out into a sticky silence. No dogs barking, no people sounds. Even the chickens in the coop were quiet. Seemed a little odd that nobody had come out by now. In the near-dusk stillness, a car approaching could be heard a long way off.

He waited a few seconds longer, then climbed the porch steps. There was an old-fashioned bell push on the jamb next to the door; he thumbed it, listened to a hollow ringing inside. It didn't bring anybody.

He tried the bell again. Then he called out, loud, "Hello the house! Anybody home?"

The stillness remained unbroken.

The pickup indicated somebody was here—if not Jerry Belsize, then one or both of his parents. Runyon went around the house to the rear. A light burned palely in one window, but there didn't seem to be much point in looking in. When he passed the wire-enclosed chicken run, one of the hens began squawking and disappeared inside the henhouse. There should've been farm-animal sounds, too—cows, horses—but he couldn't hear any. It was so quiet his steps made sharp little crunching sounds on the dry grass.

Too quiet. It felt strange to him now, as if the entire farm were holding its collective breath.

He crossed toward the smaller of the barns. Much of the daylight had gone; the sunset colors were pale fast-fading streaks, like squiggle marks made with invisible ink. Shadows lay long around the outbuildings, heavy among the trees that drooped over the stream. Nothing moved anywhere within the range of his vision.

The tractor stood near the closed barn doors. He stepped past it, tugged one door half-open, looked in at stacks of baled hay shrouded in gloom, and called out again. All that got him was a faint echo of his own voice. He closed the door, moved on to the larger barn. The doors there stood partially open. He widened the gap and leaned in. Another hail brought a stirring somewhere at the rear, then the faint nicker of a horse. That was all.

There was nobody at any of the other outbuildings, nobody over by the creek. Runyon was on cold alert by then. Something wrong here. He could feel it, like an electrical charge that acted on his nerve endings. Didn't like it because he had no idea of its cause or effect. He went to the Ford, unlocked the glove compartment, took out a flashlight and his .357 Magnum in its carry holster. He clipped the holster to his belt under the left tail of his jacket. While he was doing that he scanned the property, listening. Nothing had changed anywhere. The tableau remained breathlessly still.

He felt exposed now, even though nearly all the daylight had evaporated and dusk lay gray-black over everything in sight. His shoulders hunched as he moved around the side of the house, tension building in him as it always did when he found himself in a potentially dangerous situation. This time he lifted up on his toes to look through the lighted window. Big old-fashioned kitchen. Empty. He walked around to the back entrance. The screen door was partially ajar, the wood door behind it wide open. He eased the screen open, called out, waited through ten seconds of nothing, and stepped cautiously inside.

Cooking smells assailed him. Two pots sat on the stove top, the burners under them turned off. In an alcove beyond the window, two places had been set at a Formica-topped table; there was food on the plates, utensils and napkins awry beside them as if they had been hurriedly tossed down. The two chairs there were pulled out at angles from the tables. Runyon went to the stove. One of the pots contained a meat stew, the other water in which something had been boiled; both were still warm.

He took a quick turn through the other rooms. A couple of windows were open to let air in and the day's heat out, but there was no sign of the Belsizes or of any disturbance. Back to the kitchen. Two people interrupted while they were eating, suddenly or urgently enough to send them rushing out into a second vehicle and away from the farm. Not long before his arrival; he must have just missed them. In which case he was trespassing and the smart thing to do was get the hell out of here. None of his business. He could always come back in the morning with the subpoena.

But the feeling of wrongness persisted as he stepped outside again. Cop's instincts, seldom wrong in twenty-plus years. Instead of going to the car, he retraced his earlier path along the chicken run to the henhouse. A quick look inside with the flashlight revealed a bunch of hens and nothing else. The startled noises they made followed him across to the hay barn. He spent half a minute in there, shining the light over the dirt floor and the stacked bales.

The larger barn's cavernous interior was spotted with farm equipment, a stack of lumber, odds and ends. At the far end were a pair of doors, one open and the other closed. The closed one would lead to the stable where he'd heard the horse earlier. The open one . . . tack room, probably. He moved in that direction, playing the light in front of him, his right hand on the butt of his weapon.

When he neared the door he pulled up short, listening. Faint sound from somewhere close by. It took him a few seconds to identify it: a kind of slow, rhythmic creaking. The tack room? He went ahead again, heel and toe until he reached the tack room door. It opened inward; he shoved it wide, at the same time swinging the flash beam inside. What it picked out of the darkness froze him, made him blink and stare.

In the middle of the room a man hung suspended from a rope looped over a thick crossbeam.

Runyon had seen a lot of death in his time, all kinds, but none quite like this. The unexpectedness, the incongruity, threw him off balance. The hanged man was Latino, slight, fortyish, wearing Levi's and a khaki workshirt. His

lined face was the color of blackened liver, tongue showing at one mouth corner, eyes popped and reflecting the
glare like rounds of glass. Wound on the side of his head,
black with drying blood. The rope, a thick hemp stretched
taut and tied off around a ring in the wall, bit so deeply
into his flesh that it was only partially visible below the
chin. A vagrant breeze through an open sidewall window
stirred the body just enough to cause the creaking.

He swept the light off the dead man, around the narrow room, down across the floor. No signs of a struggle,
nothing disturbed. But it wasn't a suicide; there was nothing in the vicinity that the man could have stepped or
jumped off of. He'd been strung up. Murdered.

Runyon entered the room long enough to touch the
back of one dangling hand. Still warm. Not dead long.
Then he backed out of the doorway, fanning the beam
back through the barn until it picked out the open entrance doors. He held it there and followed the long
lighted path, getting his cell phone out to call 911 as he
went.

As he neared the doors, his ears picked up a rumbling
motor noise. Car coming on the farm road. He quickened
his pace. The sidespill from the oncoming headlights
brightened the darkness out there; he switched off the
torch as he came into the opening.

Movement behind him. He sensed rather than heard it,
and his reaction was instinctive and immediate. He started
to turn, started to duck away, started to drop both the

flash and the cell so he could defend himself. But there wasn't enough time for any of it.

Something whipped out of the darkness, exploded against the side of his head, and knocked him cockeyed.

4

JAKE RUNYON

He was down on all fours, crawling around in the dirt, trying to get up. At first he didn't know where he was or what had happened. Then he did, in a disjointed, urgent way, but he couldn't do anything about it because he couldn't stand up. His legs and arms felt like bloated things made of rubber. Pain pulsed and hammered through his skull. He couldn't see straight, couldn't make his thoughts connect. He kept on trying to stand up and each time he fell down again.

His ears worked all right—they were the only part of him that seemed to be functioning. Sounds all around him, engulfing him. Footsteps running away, car engine, raised voices, footsteps running toward him. He fumbled for the Magnum, couldn't find it. Tried to get up and fell down. He stayed down on all fours this time, shaking his head like a dog. His eyes were open, but all he could see was blurred images and flashes of light mixed with dark. Nausea boiled in his stomach. He never puked, he hated to puke—he leaned forward on his elbows and puked.

More voices, or the same voices, close by. Sudden stabbing light in his eyes, blinding him. He twisted his head away from it, and the motion brought a new eruption of pain. He flopped over on his side. Wetness ran along his cheek, trickled into the corner of his mouth. Blood.

"Who is he?"

"Never saw him before."

"Oh, my Lord, look at his head!"

"Somebody must've hit him . . . board there's got blood on it."

". . . Jerry?"

"His car's not here."

Words clogged in Runyon's throat; he spit out some of them like gobs of phlegm. ". . . Dead man . . . police . . ."

"What's he saying?"

"Can't understand him."

"John, look there, under his coat . . . he has a gun!"

"Christ! Here, hold the flashlight."

Hands on him, fumbling at his waist. First rule of law enforcement: Never let anybody take your weapon. He fought the hands, or tried to. Too strong. His numb fingers scrabbled over the empty holster. Brains scrambled, unarmed, helpless.

"What's he doing here? What happened to him?"

"How the hell should I know?"

"Don't snap at me, John."

More words came out of Runyon's throat. ". . . Dead man . . . hanging . . ."

"Did you hear that? 'Dead man'! Oh, my God—Jerry!"

"Jerry's not here. You didn't see his car, did you?"

". . . Tack room . . ."

"John?"

"I heard it. Listen, he needs a doctor. You go in the house, call nine-eleven, tell them to send deputies and an ambulance. I'll check the tack room."

"You be careful."

"Go on, Dora; hurry."

The light went away. So did running steps in two directions. Runyon pulled one knee under him. The bloated, rubbery feeling was starting to go away. Tingling sensation in his hands now. He reached up to swab at the wetness on his cheek, probe along the side of his head. Soft spot on the temple, blood-wet. Puffed ear. All of that registered without meaning or implication.

He lifted his head and shook it again. When the bright pain subsided this time, he could see a little more clearly. Shapes swam through his vision, settled, and he was looking at one of the open barn doors. He crawled toward it, got both hands on the edge, found the strength to lift himself along the door edge until he was upright. He clung there, blinking, looking into the barn, waiting for the light to come back.

Whoever had blindsided him had been hiding near the

doors, behind the stack of lumber. Long gone now. Whose voices? John and Dora—the Belsizes, Jerry's parents, returned home. He could remember and reason that much. He tried to put more of it together. Nothing else would come. Pain pulsed up sharp again; his head felt like a firebox.

The flash beam reappeared, came bobbing toward him. Picked him out and held on him from a short distance away. He shut his eyes tight against the glare.

"You just stand there, mister. I still got that gun of yours." Then, angrily, "Who did that to Manuel? You?"

He tried to say no. All that came out was a grunt.

"Who, then? Same one busted your head?"

Another grunt. Affirmative.

"Manuel . . . God Almighty, he never harmed nobody in his life. Who'd want to do a thing like that to him? It don't make sense."

Grunt. Grunt. Like a goddamn Neanderthal.

"Who are you, mister? What're you doing on my farm?"

Runyon worked spit through his mouth, struggling to concentrate. He formed words in his mind, pushed one of them out. "Pocket."

"What?"

And then the rest: "Inside . . . jacket . . . pocket."

A hand reached through the light, fumbled with his jacket. Found his ID case, yanked it out, flipped it open.

"Private investigator? What the hell?"

He wanted to say "subpoena," but he couldn't get his mouth around the word. He grunted again instead.

"Crazy," Belsize said. "Just plain crazy. First the fires, now this. Chrissake, what's going on around here?"

Runyon let go of the door, first one hand, then the other. He could stand all right, but he couldn't walk yet. Two wobbly steps and his knees sagged; he would've collapsed if Belsize hadn't grabbed him and held him up.

"Take it easy, mister. Just sit down here until the ambulance comes."

"No. Walk."

"Better not try it."

"Walk. Move."

". . . All right then. Lean on me."

Belsize slid a muscled arm around him and they walked, slow, across the yard. His first few steps were clumsy, but on the way the last of the bloated feeling left his legs and his equilibrium came back. As they neared the farmhouse, ablaze with light now, he felt he could walk on his own. He pushed out of Belsize's grasp and tried it. A little stagger, but otherwise okay.

He made it as far as the porch steps, sat down on one of them. Belsize left him there and went inside the house. Voices drifted out to him that he didn't try to listen to. Most of his senses were working again, but the disorientation wouldn't right itself, wouldn't let him think. The strain of trying made his head hurt even more.

Wait. Just sit here and wait.

He was feeling better until the noisy parade started. Sirens, red and blue flashers, glaring headlights. Ambulance, sheriff's department cruisers, other cars filling up the farm-yard. People milling around, talking in loud voices. More confusion that rekindled the fire in the firebox.

The EMTs took one good look at him and made him lie down on a stretcher. They checked his vital signs, and one of them mopped up the blood and put something stinging on his head wound while the other asked the usual questions: What's your name? What day is it? Do you know where you are? How many fingers am I holding up? He answered them all right, but the response time was slow—a mental delay between hearing them and pro-cessing and voicing the answers. He could talk well enough now, with only a little slur to the words, but his thoughts still wouldn't connect. Scrambled him up good, whoever had clobbered him.

One of the sheriff's deputies, or maybe the sheriff himself, came over and threw some hard questions at him about the dead man in the tack room. Officious type, jut-jawed, one hand resting on the butt of his ser-vice revolver. Runyon's slow responses didn't satisfy him; the questions came faster, overlapping what he was trying to say. It made him angry. He might have said something harsh if the EMTs hadn't intervened. Talk to the man later, one of them said, after the ER docs get a look at him. Which hospital? Red Bluff General, where else?

He didn't want to go to a hospital. Practically lived in hospitals during Colleen's illness, hated the damn places.

But the EMTs wouldn't listen to any argument. One of them said, "You don't have a choice, man. Head injury's nothing to fool around with, not for you, not for us." They loaded him into the ambulance, and away they went, bouncing over the uneven farm road.

Good thing they didn't use the siren on this trip. The ride was long enough and bad enough without the scream of a siren to make it a rolling nightmare.

At the hospital the first thing they did as they were wheeling him in was take his wallet. Sure, right—find out if he had any medical insurance. More questions from a woman in scrubs, one about notification. Was there anyone he wanted notified of his "accident" and where he was? No, he said. Joshua wouldn't care, and why burden Bill or Tamara with a nonagency matter?

More poking and prodding in the ER, amid the hospital stink of medicine and sickness and death, the humming and chirping machines, and the sudden cries that made your skin crawl. Kill himself before he died like Colleen had, in a place like this. But that wasn't going to happen. He wasn't terminal yet, just fuzzy, confused. He managed to summon the will to shut himself down, just let it all happen. Heard somebody say, "Skull doesn't appear to be fractured. Vitals are strong. Eyes seem mostly clear." Heard somebody else say, "Let's get him to X-ray," and off he went to have his head examined.

After that, they put him in a ward room with three

other beds, all of them occupied, and rolled a curtain around him. A nurse came in and hooked him up to an IV and fed in some kind of sedative. He didn't mind. The sooner he was rid of tonight, the better. . . .

5

I had the white gift box under my arm when I walked into the condo. Kerry was curled up on the living room couch with a book and Shameless, the world's laziest cat. When she saw the box she said with mock excitement, "For me? You shouldn't have."

"I didn't," I said. "It's not for you."

"Aha. One of your other women."

"The only other woman in my life is Emily, and it's not for her, either."

I set the box on the coffee table, went over to kiss her. She'd put on fresh makeup, brushed her auburn hair to a silky gloss. She looked good and tasted good, and I told her so.

"I feel good," she said. "The checkup did wonders for my spirits."

"You didn't try to do too much today?"

"No. Worked for a while, took a nap, had a long talk

with Cybil on the phone. Oh, and Paula stopped by for a few minutes. She brought me this book."

Paula was Paula Hanley, an interior designer friend of Kerry's and a grade-A flake. To put it mildly. Among Paula's none too endearing traits was a certainty that what was good for her was also good for everybody else; she mounted conversion campaigns at every opportunity. This was compounded by the fact that she was a faddist who believed passionately, at least for a while, in any hare-brained new or old concept that came into current vogue. Scientology, Est, New Age tantric sex, holistic medicine, and most recently, God help us, some sort of weird off-shoot of the Haitian voodoo religion.

"Don't tell me," I said as I sat down beside Kerry. "Let me guess. It's a book about health and well-being through voodoo ritual. All you have to do is dance naked to the beat of drums and you'll be good as new."

"Hah."

"Sacrifice a goat? Stick pins in a doll that looks like your worst enemy?"

She held up the book so I could read the title and author. *The Magic Island* by W. B. Seabrook.

"Uh-huh," I said.

"It's not what you think," she said. "It's an early history of Haitian voodoo practices, first published in 1929 — native accounts of all sorts of rituals and ceremonies, not to mention encounters with werewolves, zombies, and fire hags."

"Terrific. In other words, pure fiction."

"A lot of it is superstition, yes. Paula doesn't think so, but to me it's entertainment. I'm enjoying it."

"Don't tell me she just dropped it off without the usual proselytizing?"

"More or less."

"Not even an invitation to watch a priest behead a chicken?"

"No, and don't put her down—she's been a good friend through all of this."

"Sorry. I know she has. But I can't help remembering all the past lunacies."

"Of course," Kerry said musingly, "there are some fascinating possibilities in voodoo rites. I could dress in a red robe, wear a hat in the shape of horns, carry a whip and a votive candle, and make an offering of food, drink, and money to Papa Legba, Baron Samedi, and the other voodoo gods while a *bocor* chants over a cemetery grave. That's been known to cure all sorts of illnesses."

I stared at her. "You're kidding, right?"

"Not at all," she said, and her mouth twitched and she burst out laughing. God, it was good to hear her laugh again. "You should see the look on your face."

". . . Had me going there for a second."

She put the book down and gave me a long look that I couldn't quite read. But her eyes were soft. "Another thing I've been doing today is thinking," she said.

"About what?"

"That I haven't been much good to you the past few months."

"You're always good to me. And good for me."

"You know what I mean."

"No, I don't."

"Sex," she said.

"Hey, where did that come from? That's not important right now."

"You're a man, aren't you?"

"A sixty-two-year-old man. At my age—"

"Oh, don't give me that age nonsense. You're as horny as you ever were. So am I, in spirit. I haven't lost interest any more than you have."

"Sure, but under the circumstances . . ."

"The circumstances. I'm tired of letting 'the circumstances' rule our lives. Admit it—you want us to be the way we were as much as I do."

"Of course I do, but—"

"And that means making love again."

"Kerry . . . why are we having this conversation?"

"Why do you think we're having it?"

"The timing isn't right. . . ."

"No, not quite. But pretty soon. If I'm well enough to go back to work week after next, I'm well enough to start having a love life again."

She had that look she gets when she's made up her mind about something. The look she'd had all through the surgery and radiation therapy. Very determined woman, Kerry. She accuses me of being stubborn sometimes, but she can be just as hardheaded.

"I don't know," I said. "You don't want to do anything that might—"

"Might what? Give us both some pleasure?"

"I mean . . . what would Dr. Janek say?"

"I don't discuss my sex life with my oncologist, for heaven's sake."

"Uh . . . the radiation burn . . ."

"We'll be careful."

"Still, the contact, the pressure, close like that . . ."

"Resourceful, aren't we? We'll think of something when the time comes."

The conversation was making me uncomfortable. By way of changing the subject, I went out to the kitchen for a bottle of Anchor Steam. When I came back, Kerry had picked up *The Magic Island,* but she wasn't reading—she was eyeing the gift box again over the top of the book.

"Okay," she said. "What's in the box?"

"An investigation I let myself get talked into today."

"You're investigating a box?"

"For starters, yes. Whether or not it goes any further depends on what I find in there—and what Tamara finds on some computer discs that I off-loaded to her."

"Sounds exciting."

"My kind of case, these days."

I explained about Celeste Ogden's hatred and distrust of her brother-in-law, and her suspicion that her sister's death wasn't accidental, and what she'd hinted I would find among Nancy Mathias's personal effects.

"She may be right about Mathias," Kerry said. "When a woman feels that strongly and intuitively about a person, there's usually some basis for it."

"Maybe. Unless she's as monomaniacal as she claims Mathias is."

"Well, why don't we have a look in the box?"

"We?"

"There might be something a woman would pick up on that a man wouldn't. Did Tamara go through the contents?"

"No. I figured the discs were enough of a burden. I'd've tackled the diary myself, but you know how I am with computers."

"I don't envy her the job. Reading another person's private diary is a kind of invasion, even if the woman is dead."

"And pawing through the rest of her effects isn't?"

"Not exactly. It's not quite the same thing." She laid the book aside and sat up. "*The Magic Island* isn't all that interesting, and frankly, I'm bored just sitting around. If you don't want my help, I think I'll go in and do some more work."

"I want your help," I said.

So we hunkered over the box like a pair of grave robbers and divvied up the contents. One thing became apparent immediately: Nancy Mathias had been something of a pack rat, saving everything, including handwritten notes to and from her husband. I looked through the notes first. There were a fair number, mostly written by her, a few of them crumpled as if they'd been thrown away and she'd rescued them. The usual "gone to the store, be back in half an hour"—all except one. That one said:

> Darling,
> Im going to spend the weekend in CV, I need to be by myself. Please dont be angry. And please meet me at Ds at 2:00 on Tuesday. Please! I cant deal with this alone.
>
> N

I showed the note to Kerry. She said, "Deal with what alone, I wonder."

"Could be just about anything."

"She sounds desperate. And begging. Three 'pleases.'"

"Which could mean Mathias wasn't or hadn't been responsive to whatever it was. That would fit with what Celeste Ogden says about him—cold, self-involved, controlling."

"Assuming 'Darling' was her husband," Kerry said.

"Pretty safe assumption."

"No way to tell when it was written. Can you find out?"

"Maybe, if we can figure out what or who 'CV' and 'D' stand for."

Insurance policies next. House, two cars, joint term life, all of them with Pacific Rim Insurance. The death benefit amount on the life policy was $50,000, with the Mathiases as each other's beneficiary. There was a double indemnity clause, which made the payoff to Brandon Mathias $100,000. That was a lot of money to me; to the head of a multi-million-dollar computer software company it was more in the category of chump change. No motive for murder there—unless Mathias was so overextended for one reason or another that he desperately needed a hundred grand bailout money. Not too likely, but worth checking. If we continued with the investigation, the first thing we'd have to do was look into his entire financial background.

Kerry said, "Here's something."

She'd been poring through packets of canceled checks from the current year, and had pulled out one from the Mathiases' joint Calvert Group investment account. The amount on it was $10,000, dated three weeks ago and made out to T. R. Quentin.

"That's a lot of money for one check," she said.

"Yes, it is."

"None of the other checks in this account or her Washington Mutual account come even close to that amount. No others made out to T. R. Quentin, either."

I made a note of the name, date, amount, and check number. "Let's see if there's anything among the rest of this stuff to explain the ten thousand."

There wasn't. Whether T. R. Quentin was an individual or a company of some kind, neither the name nor the initials appeared anywhere else in the records. Kerry, being thorough, checked to see how many checks had been made out to individuals; there were a dozen or so, most to Philomena Ruiz, the cleaning woman, and none for more than $300.

I shuffled through the various bill receipts, all of which were marked "paid" in the same hand that had written the "Darling" note. Nancy Mathias had paid her bills promptly, by both check and computer transfer, and they all looked to be routine—utilities, household expenses, credit card charges, women's clothing shops, doctor, dentist, house cleaner, gardener, pool service. There were no invoices from lawyers, psychiatrists, or private detective agencies to indicate dissatisfaction, unrest, or suspicion on her part.

One of two property tax bills solved the CV question. The Mathiases owned a second home in Carmel Valley, valued for tax purposes at $350,000. Some second home. But it was a piker compared to their primary Palo Alto residence; that one was worth a million two. Both homes were held jointly. Not that it would have made a difference if she'd been sole owner; they'd have been part of the inheritance package in any case.

There were three Ds among the canceled checks— Delborn Florists, Denise's Designs, Drovnik Gardening Service. The second was an exclusive dress shop in Atherton—exclusive because of the prices they charged for an "evening suit" and an unspecified lingerie item. Didn't seem to be any possible connection between any of them and the pleading urgency in the note.

"Is this all of Nancy Mathias's personal records?" Kerry asked when we were done.

"Everything that was in her office desk, evidently."

"Poor woman. Her sister was right—she really did lead

a closed-off life. No letters or photographs or scrapbook items, nothing to indicate she had any friends. Not even a calendar or datebook."

"Even if Mathias forced reclusiveness on her, that doesn't mean he had her killed."

"There might be something in her diary."

"It would have to be pretty compelling," I said. "So far I just don't see motive or anything else to justify the kind of investigation Celeste Ogden wants."

6

JAKE RUNYON

Except for a headache, a swollen ear, and a dry mouth, he was all right in the morning. Unscrambled, in command of himself again. He could remember everything that had happened at the Belsize farm up to the moment he'd been assaulted. The rest of it was blurred and fragmentary, like images from a particularly vivid dream.

A nurse came in and the first thing he asked her, in a croak that didn't sound much like his own voice, was how soon he could get out of there. Not until Dr. Yeng examined him, she said. When would that be? On Doctor's regular rounds this morning. She gave Runyon some water, took his temperature, checked his pulse. He asked if he had a concussion and she confirmed it. How serious? He'd have to speak to Dr. Yeng about that. The only information Runyon could get out of her was that three stitches had been necessary to close the wound on his temple. He asked where his clothes and belongings were. Clothing in a locker, valuables in a lockbox. He talked her into fetching the valuables bag. The subpoena was there; so were his wallet and cell phone. The .357 Magnum and his license case were missing. Sheriff's people had them, likely. Better have.

The doctor didn't show up until after eleven, and by then the antiseptic white walls were beginning to close in on him. Young, Asian, efficient. Dr. Yeng studied the chart, then asked questions while he shined a light in Runyon's eyes and examined his bandaged temple and cauliflower ear. Had he suffered loss of consciousness after the blow to his head? No. Nausea? Some. Disorientation, dizziness, clumsiness, slow to respond to questions? All of the above, but all gone now.

Yeng seemed satisfied. "Your concussion appears relatively mild," he said. "The X-rays showed no skull fracture or brain hemorrhage or evidence of blood clots. You're fortunate you weren't hit any harder."

"I guess I am."

"Have you had any kind of head trauma before last night?"

"No."

"All to the good. Do you know anything about concussions?"

"A little, not much."

Dr. Yeng took that as an invitation to deliver a brief technical lecture. After such a trauma, he said, the arteries in the brain constrict, reducing blood flow and lowering the rate at which oxygen is delivered to the brain. At the same time the demand rises for sugar glucose to provide energy to the brain for healing, but the narrowed arteries are unable to meet the demand; this creates a metabolic crisis, requiring time for the brain to correct the chemical imbalance and the damaged cells to repair themselves. How much time varies with the severity of the trauma, and the individual person's health and how well he takes care of himself during the healing process. In Runyon's case, if he was careful and no complications developed, the time should be relatively short.

"Avoid strenuous activity; get plenty of rest," Yeng said. "If any symptoms should recur—severe headaches, dizziness, double vision, a blackout lasting even a few seconds—you need to see your physician without delay."

"Understood. Can I get out of here now?"

"I don't see why not, as long as you're feeling up to it. After you've seen your visitors."

He'd been expecting that. "Law officers?"

"That's right. They're waiting outside."

"Send them in."

There were two of them. One brain, one brawn. The brain was in his fifties, short, compact, with sparse sandy hair and a quiet manner, dressed in a suit and tie; his name was Rinniak and he was a special investigator with the county sheriff's department. The brawn, Kelso, wore a deputy's uniform with knife-crease trousers and starched blouse and a Sam Browne belt so well oiled the leather gleamed in the room lights. Bulky, thick-necked, red-faced—half a foot taller and half a yard wider than Rinniak and, judging from his blue starry eyes, about half as intelligent. Kelso seemed vaguely familiar, but Runyon couldn't place him until he took up an aggressive stance at the foot of the bed, a hand resting lightly on the butt of his service revolver. Right. The one who'd thrown questions at him last night. Deputy in charge of the Gray's Landing substation, and the kind of suspicious, hard-nosed veteran who resented private sector investigators—the kind you could have trouble with even if you were careful around him.

Rinniak sat in one of the two chairs. He said, "We'll try to keep this brief, Mr. Runyon. Can you remember what happened last night?"

"Everything before I got blindsided."

"That's what we're interested in."

Kelso said, "How about you start by telling us what a San Francisco private cop was doing at the Belsize farm."

"Delivering a subpoena. Or trying to."

"Who to?"

"Gerald Belsize."

The sheriff's men exchanged glances. "What kind of case?" Rinniak asked.

"Assault and robbery. Belsize was a witness."

"Where and when?"

"Three months ago, in San Francisco. He took his girlfriend down there for the weekend and the two of them—"

"What girlfriend?" Kelso demanded. "You mean Sandra Parnell?"

"That's right."

The outthrust jaw tightened. "I should've known she was that way."

"What way?"

"Cheap. Decent girls don't spend out-of-town weekends with their boyfriends."

Add prude to suspicious and hard-nosed.

Rinniak said, "Go ahead, Mr. Runyon."

"Belsize and Parnell were at a SoMa nightclub. On the way out she stopped to use the bathroom and he went on to the parking lot. Spotted two men beating up on a third, stealing his wallet. One of them came after him and he ran back to the club."

"Yeah, that figures," Kelso said. "Pure coward."

"The mugger had a knife. You don't have to be a coward to run from cold steel."

"I know him. You don't."

Runyon said, "Belsize claimed he couldn't describe either mugger, but the girl said he told her later that he got a good look at the one with the knife—he just didn't want to get involved."

"That figures, too."

"SFPD arrested a felon named Zander as one of the perps. He had the victim's wallet in his possession. He swears he's innocent, claims he found the wallet half a block away. His lawyer contacted Belsize, got no cooperation, so he called my agency to check him out and deliver a subpoena. Routine business."

"The girl didn't tell us about any of that," Kelso said to Rinniak.

"No reason for her to. It's not germane."

"Still should've told us."

Rinniak asked, "How did Belsize check out?"

"Clean."

"Wrong," Kelso said. "He's been trouble his whole life. Only a matter of time before he got into the big time."

"If you say so."

"I say so. You never met him, huh?"

"No."

"Anybody else in his family?"

"Not before last night."

"How about Manuel Silvera?"

"I don't know anybody named Manuel Silvera."

"Belsize's hired hand. Man you found beaten and strung up in the barn. You did find him, right? Poking around in there where you didn't belong. Trespassing."

Rinniak gave him an irritated look. The brawn had a knack for rubbing people wrong, his coworkers included. "Let him tell it, Don."

"Sure, sure. So tell it, Runyon."

He told it, leaving nothing out except for his walk-through of the farmhouse. No point in giving Kelso something else to use against him.

"So instead of leaving, you just started prowling around.

That what you usually do when you go onto private property and nobody's home?"

"No. I had a feeling something was wrong."

"A feeling. Sure."

"Every cop I ever knew was sensitive that way," Runyon said. "You walk into a situation, it doesn't feel right, your instincts take over. Sixth sense. You don't have it, Deputy?"

Kelso scowled at him. Rinniak said, "So you went around back and looked through the kitchen window."

"That's right. Just checking. Half-eaten dinner on the table, chairs pulled out—it looked as though the people had left in a hurry."

"They had a phone call. Anonymous. The caller said their son, Jerry, had been in an accident down by Orford and they better come immediately. You missed them leaving by maybe ten minutes."

"Lured away so Silvera could be attacked?"

"That's how it looks."

Kelso said, "This feeling got real strong then, huh? Led you straight to the tack room in the barn."

"Not quite. I went to my car for my weapon and a flashlight. It was dusk by then and I—"

"Why'd you figure you needed a gun?"

Runyon mustered patience, kept his face empty and his voice even. "I didn't figure I'd need it. But I was a police officer in Seattle for a dozen years and I've been in enough bad situations not to take any chances. You know my background by now. You've got my license—you must've run a check on me."

"We ran one," Rinniak said. "Spotless record."

"Yeah, spotless," Kelso said.

"Don, for Christ's sake, let me handle this, will you?" He gestured to Runyon to go on.

"I checked the hay barn first, then the big barn. No real cause to enter either one except that feeling. For all I knew somebody was hurt somewhere on the property. I was in the big barn when I heard a creaking sound. That's what led me to the tack room and the dead man. I was on my way outside to call nine-eleven when I got clobbered."

"Where do you suppose the assailant was all this time?"

"Hiding. Probably behind the stack of lumber. It was a board he hit me with, wasn't it?"

"Two-by-two. You didn't have any idea he was still there?"

"I should've figured he might be, but I didn't. Window in the tack room was open and I made the wrong assumption."

"You didn't manage to catch a glimpse of him before he hit you?"

"Happened too quick."

"Anything that might help identify him?"

"No. Too dark in the barn." Runyon's mouth was dry again. He drank from the half-full glass on the bedside table. "Can I ask you a question?"

"Go ahead."

"The motive. Why string a man up like that, a hired hand? Why lure the family away to do it?"

"No ideas that make any sense. Silvera was a family man himself, quiet, steady, no trouble to anybody that we can find—least likely candidate for premeditated homicide you can imagine."

"There isn't any motive," Kelso said. "Psycho firebugs don't need reasons for what they do."

Runyon said, "Firebug?"

"Three fires of suspicious origin in and around Gray's Landing this summer," Rinniak told him. "Junior high school, old Odd Fellows lodge building, abandoned barn. No fatalities or injuries, fortunately—all empty the nights they were torched. We've ruled out arson for gain in each case. And three's too many in too short a time to be coincidence."

"Firebugs don't usually change their M.O. and start hanging people."

"They do if they're crazy enough," Kelso said. "It's none of your concern anyhow, Runyon."

The throbbing ache in Runyon's head said differently. But there was no gain in arguing with a man like Kelso; it would only make him more belligerent. He said to Rinniak, "If it's all right with you, I'd like my license and my weapon back as soon as possible."

"No problem. You can pick them up at the Gray's Landing substation."

"How about my car?"

"Still at the Belsize farm. When did the doctor say you could be released?"

"As soon as I talked to you."

"Well, if it doesn't take too long, I'll wait and give you a ride down. You feel up to driving to your motel?"

"I can manage."

"Better plan to spend the weekend. Rest up, keep available in case we need to talk to you again."

"I was planning on it anyway. I still haven't done the job I came here to do."

Kelso laughed, a surprisingly effeminate sound from such a cowboy. "Deliver a subpoena to Jerry Belsize? I wouldn't worry about that if I were you."

"No?"

"No. Belsize won't be testifying at any trial in San Francisco. He'll be in jail awaiting trial himself once we find him. *He's* the psycho who set those fires and strung up Manny Silvera."

7

JAKE RUNYON

Jerry Belsize had been missing for more than twenty-four hours. Last seen at around 9:00 A.M. yesterday, in the company of the murdered hired man, Manuel Silvera. He'd left the farm shortly afterward, supposedly for his job at a feed mill in Orford, but he hadn't shown up there or called in with an excuse. His parents had no idea why he'd skipped work or where he'd gone. He was supposed to have been back at the farm in time for supper; that was why the Belsizes had panicked when they got the anonymous phone call. Sandra Parnell claimed she hadn't heard from him and had no idea where he might be. According to the victim's wife, Silvera told her by phone that he'd be home late because he had "extra work and something else to do" at the Belsize farm. He hadn't said what the something else was.

A search of the big barn had turned up two empty one-gallon kerosene cans hidden in the hayloft. And a search of Jerry Belsize's room yielded all the components for the kind of simple timing device used in each of the three fires. Circumstantial evidence, but fairly damning just the same.

Runyon learned all of this on the drive down to Gray's Landing. Unlike the deputy, Kelso, Joe Rinniak was an evenhanded man—forthcoming, and respectful of an ex–Seattle cop with Runyon's credentials. He seemed to need to unload to an understanding ear.

The operating theory, the one Kelso subscribed to, was that Silvera had seen the kid setting one of the blazes and kept quiet about it because he didn't want to get involved, or maybe for blackmail purposes. That was the alleged motive for the hanging—to make sure Silvera stayed silent. Why make his kill on his own home ground? He was a psychotic, not thinking rationally. Why disappear? Runyon showing up, almost catching him in the act, had panicked him and sent him on the run.

"We've got a BOLO out on him right now," Rinniak said. "Kelso wanted a fugitive warrant, but I don't think we have enough for that yet. Belsize doesn't have any money to speak of and he's not overly bright—where's he going to go that he won't be caught? Once we have him in custody and question him in detail, then we'll see."

"Sounds like you have your doubts about his guilt."

"Doubts, yes." He glanced sideways at Runyon. "You know much about pyromania?"

"Some. I handled a couple of firebug cases when I was

on the Seattle PD. You're convinced that's the kind of case it is?"

"Where the fires are concerned, what else?"

"Could be a grudge thing. Somebody with a mad-on for the community."

"That's possible, I suppose," Rinniak said, "but it doesn't fit Jerry Belsize. No cause to torch the school or the Odd Fellows hall or the Adamson barn. Looks to me like they were random targets. That argues for the firebug explanation, only he doesn't seem to fit there, either. You investigated him. What's your opinion?"

That was the main reason Rinniak was being so candid; he wanted Runyon's input. "On paper he doesn't seem to fit the profile."

"Except for the fact that he's young. Most firebugs come from poor environments, broken or dysfunctional homes—adore their mothers, hate their fathers. Repressed loners with low intelligence, low self-esteem, emotional retardation, deep-seated sexual hang-ups. Setting fires is a substitute for the sex act, the shrinks say. Gets them excited, temporarily relieves the sexual tension. But it doesn't last, so they keep on doing it."

Runyon started to nod. The steady throb in his head changed his mind.

"Belsize had a normal upbringing, and seems to be anything but sexually repressed. He's had a string of girl-friends ranging back to when he was about fourteen."

Runyon said, "Not every bug is a textbook case. Some have other problems, other motives."

"But you'd think that if Belsize was one of those, there'd be something in his background to hint at it. Sure, he's had some brushes with authority, but it's all been pretty minor stuff—two speeding tickets, a public scuffle, driving with an open beer in the car. He's got a decent job; his employer likes him; he seems to fit into the community at large. So why would he all of a sudden go off on a crazy spree this summer—setting fires, committing homicide?"

"Simmering under the surface all along."

"That's possible, sure. All firebugs are potential murderers, so the experts claim, whether they fit the profile or not. But here's another thing. Belsize comes from a solid home and has always gotten along with his folks. Seems to've gotten along with Manuel Silvera, too. Doesn't make sense to me that he'd beat and hang a man in his own backyard. Psychos don't do it that way, unless they're the kind that take out their entire families and then themselves. They set their fires and make their kills somewhere else."

"If Belsize is innocent, those kerosene cans and the timer material were plants. Who'd want to do him that much harm?"

"Good question. On the surface, he's an unlikely target. Everybody I've talked to likes the kid."

"Except Kelso," Runyon said.

"Yes. Except Kelso."

"Sounded to me as if he's got it in for Belsize."

"I think maybe he has. There's a personal angle—he's a

single father with a daughter not too long out of high school. Ashley's the rebellious type. She went against his wishes and dated Belsize on the sly for a while last year. Kelso caught them in some heavy breathing one afternoon and literally kicked the kid out of his house. Slapped him around in front of Ashley and two of their neighbors. If Belsize is guilty, why didn't he torch Kelso's house or the substation instead of a couple of public buildings and a barn?"

"Afraid of the man, maybe. Vented himself on others' property instead."

"That's a stretch, seems to me."

"Is Kelso as hard-nosed as he seems?"

"And then some. Runs his office with an iron fist. He wouldn't give his own mother a break if he caught her jaywalking."

"Maybe he was hassling Belsize. Or the real perp, if the kid's innocent. Hound somebody enough, he might just go off the deep end."

"I'd hate it if that's what's behind these crimes. Don's hard and stubborn, but he has a good record. If he overstepped himself, the entire sheriff's department will suffer for it."

They'd reached the Gray's Landing exit. As they rolled along the road into town, Rinniak said, "Might as well stop at the station and pick up your belongings now. Be quicker if I'm along."

The substation was in an old Spanish-style building across from an oak-shaded park. There were no security barriers when you walked in, just an open office with a countertop bisecting it a few paces from the door. Runyon wondered if Kelso knew how good he had it up here in the country. Probably didn't care, if he did. This was his town, his world. He wouldn't worry about anybody breaching it; if anything, he'd dare it to happen.

He was seated now behind a desk that had a polished top and everything on it neatly arranged, talking to a stringy middle-aged man dressed in a suit and tie. The older man was bareheaded, but from the way he stood, his entire demeanor, he might have had a hat in his hands. Oozing deference, as if he was there to beg a favor.

There was a hinged flap in the countertop; Rinniak lifted it and Runyon followed him through. "Hello, Mayor," Rinniak said to the stringy man.

"Joe. I just came to see if there was any word yet."

"We'll get him," Kelso said flatly. "Don't you worry about that."

"It can't be any too soon. The media is already sniffing around . . . there's a reporter and camera crew from Redding in town. . . ."

"I know. They were waiting for me when I got back a little while ago."

"Negative publicity. My God, it's just what we don't need."

Rinniak saw to introductions. The stringy man was Carl Battle, owner of a local hardware store and mayor of Gray's Landing. His handshake was damp and so brief his palm barely touched Runyon's. Battle oozed sweat as well as deference; his scalp, visible beneath sparse caramel-colored hair that had a dyed look in the overhead fluorescents, glistened with it. If ever a man didn't fit his name, it was this one.

He said to Runyon, "I'm sorry about what happened to you last night." As if he felt compelled to take personal responsibility. "Gray's Landing is normally a quiet, peaceful town. No crime or violence to speak of until . . . well, I guess you know about the fires. And now a murder, and the assault on you . . ."

Runyon said nothing.

"I understand your concussion isn't serious. You're feeling all right now?"

"Passable."

"We'll pay your hospital costs, of course. The county, I mean. We can authorize that, can't we, Joe?"

"I doubt it," Rinniak said.

Runyon's Magnum, license case, car keys, and flashlight were in a tagged plastic evidence bag; Kelso produced them from a file cabinet drawer, demanded that Runyon sign a release form before he turned over the bag. The deputy wore a tight, fixed expression the entire time. He wanted Runyon gone—Rinniak, too, for that matter—as much as Battle did. The difference between Kelso's reasons and the mayor's was that the deputy didn't care about negative publicity. He didn't like outside investigators, county or private, invading his territory or questioning his conclusions or taking the spotlight off him. Runyon had known cops like him before. Minor tyrants and righteous glory hounds. What Kelso wanted more than anything else was to arrest Jerry Belsize himself—be the hero, cement his authority, bring in a promotion.

Outside and moving again, Rinniak said, "You wouldn't know it from that display in there, but Carl's a good man. Civic-minded and honest. It's just that he doesn't know how to deal with a situation like this."

"He seemed afraid of Kelso."

"I don't know about afraid, but Don makes him nervous, that's for sure. Part of it's the iron fist and Carl being mild mannered. Part of it is that his son, Zach, is dating Don's daughter."

"Kelso doesn't like Zach any more than Jerry Belsize, is that it?"

"He doesn't think any man's good enough for Ashley, but he tolerates Zach. I think what worries Carl is that his son will get Ashley in trouble. There's no telling what Don would do then, given his temper and his moral and religious stance."

As they bounced along the uneven access lane to the Belsize farm, Runyon had flashback images of last night's ambulance ride. He held himself rigid on the seat to keep the ache in his head to a minimum. The place looked the same as it had yesterday, everything wilted and shimmery from the heat; the only signs of what had happened there were tire tracks on the dry ground stretching to the large barn. He felt nothing, seeing it all again. In Seattle he'd known police officers who were place sensitive—refused to revisit scenes where they'd been subjected to violence, suffered in one way or another if they did—but he'd never been afflicted with the syndrome. Places were just places to him. Now more than ever, with Colleen gone.

His Ford was parked where he'd left it, next to the dust-streaked pickup. Rinniak pulled up alongside. The farmhouse door had opened as they approached, and a slat of a man in his fifties, gray haired and gray bearded, had come out to stand on the porch, waiting. John Belsize, probably. He'd been just a voice behind the white flashlight glare last night.

Belsize stayed on the porch as they got out of the car. Rinniak said, "I want to talk to Mr. Belsize. You sure you're okay to drive?"

"Yes."

"I'll be in touch if there's any news. I made a note of your cellular number. If you don't hear from me by tomorrow night, you're free to go back to San Francisco."

"I may want to hang around a little longer. Depends on how much I'm needed at my agency."

"Your call. Try to stay out of Kelso's way if you can."

"If I can."

He found his way back to Gray's Landing. The Ford didn't have air-conditioning—he hadn't needed it in Seattle—and even with all the windows open, the heat was a weight on him by the time he reached the motel. The pain throb in his head had grown intense; his vision had gone a little smeary again at the edges.

In his room at the motel, the message light on the phone was blinking. Reporter from the Redding paper, requesting an interview. He erased the message; no mood for the media. He swallowed two of the Vicodin tablets they'd given him at the hospital, then cranked up the air conditioner to high cool, drew the drapes over the single window, stripped, and got into bed. This kind of enforced downtime grated on him, but the EMT last night and the doctor today had been adamant that you didn't mess around with head injuries. He mistrusted the medical profession on principle, even though the Seattle doctors had done all they could to save Colleen, but he believed Dr. Yeng's warning well enough.

He slept, but it wasn't a good sleep—fitful, sticky in spite of the air conditioner, dream ridden. The dreams were mostly an episodic succession of ghost images, distorted wanderings among hanged men, vehicles with flashing lights, dark-shadowed places filled with disembodied voices. But one, the last one, was clear and vivid in every detail, as were all of his dreams about Colleen.

In this one they were on their first date in Old Town. Old-fashioned Italian place, candles in Chianti bottles, checked tablecloths. Both of them a little nervous, but only because they didn't know each other well yet and each wanted to make a good impression. At ease in each other's company otherwise. Colleen leaning forward, her face lighted like a madonna's by the candle flame, saying, "I never thought I'd be going out with a cop." Him asking why not and her saying, "I've always been afraid of policemen, ever since I was a little kid. No reason, just that they

seemed so . . . don't know, authoritarian, dangerous." Him
saying, "You never have to be afraid of me." And her saying, "I know. It's just the opposite with you; you make me
feel safe." And the feeling that came over him in that moment, sudden and sharp and overwhelming—the revela-
tion that he was in love with Colleen McPhail and the
certainty that he would marry her and they would be together until death did them part.

He awoke dripping wet. Even the pillow was sodden—
sweat, drool, tears. But his headache had dulled and except
for a desert mouth and throat he felt better. A thin strip of
fading daylight showed where the window drapes didn't
quite overlap; his watch said it was twenty of eight. In the
bathroom he drank three glasses of water, checked the
bandage in the mirror, then took a long, careful shower.
He was hungry by the time he finished dressing. Another
good sign.

Still hot when he stepped outside and crossed to the
coffee shop. Cool enough inside, though. Noisy. He sat at
the counter, ordered iced tea and a sandwich. He was just
finishing up when somebody sat down beside him and
said, "Mr. Runyon? Can I talk to you?"

Young woman, early twenties. Short ginger blond hair.
Pale blue eyes. Pretty enough in a conventional way. Wearing shorts, a tank top, and an intense, nervous expression.

He said, "Depends on who you are."

"Sandra Parnell. Jerry's friend . . . Jerry Belsize."

"What can I do for you?"

"Not here. You're staying at the motel, right? Can't we go to your room?"

That made him wary. She didn't look cheap or duplicitous—just an average small-town young woman worried about her boyfriend—but it paid to be cautious. One of the most vicious jackrolling hookers he'd encountered in Seattle had been a sixteen-year-old with a face like an angel. "I don't think so."

"Outside, then. My car's in the lot. Please?"

There was still some daylight left and there were plenty of people around. He was still wary but curious enough to say, "All right."

Sandra Parnell went out first, stood waiting until he paid the check and joined her. "Over here," she said, and led him to a beat-up Chrysler at least as old as she was. Convertible, with the top down. He waited for her to get in before he went around to the passenger side.

She said, "Jerry's father says you're a detective. That you came up here to see Jerry about that mugging in San Francisco."

"That's right."

"He's not a bad person, Mr. Runyon. I mean, he shouldn't have lied about getting a good look at the man with the knife, but he was scared. He's scared a lot; he just can't help it."

Runyon said nothing.

"He and Manuel, they always got along. He just couldn't've done what they're saying."

"Why tell me?"

"Nobody else will listen. The cops . . . Deputy Kelso. You know him?"

"We've met."

"He kept trying to make me tell him where Jerry is. He hates Jerry because . . . never mind why; he just does. If he ever gets his hands on him . . ."

"What do you think would happen?"

"He'd beat him up. Maybe even kill him."

"He'd have to be the one to catch Jerry first."

"You think he couldn't? He knows this county like nobody else."

"Does that mean Jerry's still in the county?"

"I didn't say that."

"But you do know where he is."

"No!" Too quick, too emphatic. She knew, all right.

"The best thing for him to do," Runyon said, "is to walk himself into the county sheriff's office and talk to Joe Rinniak. He's the man in charge, not Kelso. The longer Jerry stays away, the worse it's going to look for him."

"They'd just arrest him and convict him and send him to prison. They wouldn't keep looking for the real criminal."

"Is that what you believe?"

"It's what Jerry believes."

"You need hard evidence to convict a man of arson and murder, Sandra. There's no hard evidence against him."

"What about those kerosene cans and the stuff in his room?"

"Circumstantial. No direct links to any of the fires. Or to the murder of the hired hand. Can he prove where he was when that went down?"

"He was with me." Too quick again. A lie this time.

"All day yesterday? Why didn't he go home when he was supposed to?"

"I can't tell you that."

"Why can't you?"

"I just can't."

"Let's quit playing around. You think he should turn himself in. If you didn't, you wouldn't be here talking to me."

She made a snuffling sound, rubbed at her nose, her eyes. "It doesn't matter what I want. I can't make Jerry do anything—he's too scared."

"Neither can I, if that's what you're after."

"But maybe you—"

What caused her to break off was the roar of engine exhaust as a car came fast-wheeling into the lot. It racketed down the aisle behind them, a low-slung yellow and black Trans Am; slowed, and then slid into the empty space close on Runyon's side.

Sandra said, "Oh shit."

The Trans Am's driver, a girl about Sandra's age, shut off the noise and managed to squeeze herself out of the car without her door scraping the Chrysler's. Slender, with oversized breasts in a tight bra under a loose blouse; midnight dark hair flowing down silkily to the curve of tight-denimed buttocks. Her passenger was slower to emerge.

He stood peering over the cartop, a lanky kid with a mop of caramel-colored hair.

"Hey there," the girl said to Sandra. "New boyfriend?"

"Shut up, Ashley."

"No, he's that detective, right? I can tell by the bandage. How's your head?" she asked Runyon.

"Sore."

"I'll bet. I'll bet if Jerry hit you any harder with that two-by-two, he'd've taken your head right off."

Runyon said nothing.

"Jerry didn't do it," Sandra said, wearily this time. "Not that you care one way or the other."

"That's right, I don't."

Sandra looked over at the lanky kid. "Why do you let her drive your car, Zach? She'll wreck it someday. She's a menace."

"She likes to drive fast," he said.

"She won't like if it her father catches her."

"Hah," Ashley said. She tossed her head, putting the long hair into a dark swirl. Habitual gesture, from the way she did it, showing it off. "You look all blotchy and red eyed, Sandy. Does that mean they caught Jerry?"

"You know they haven't."

"But they will. I'll bet it won't take long."

"Why don't you go squat on a sharp stick?"

"Oo, nasty. You hear what she said, Zach?"

"Yeah, I heard."

"You going to do anything about it?"

"What do you want me to do?"

Ashley laughed. "Nothing. Come on, let's go eat. I'm starving. Bye, Detective. Bye, Sandy. Try not to cry too much tonight—your complexion's not so good as it is."

The two of them went off, the girl trailing more laughter.

Sandra said, "Kelso's daughter. But I guess you figured that out."

He nodded. "And the mayor's son."

"Yeah. She's a bitch and he's a wimp. He lets her lead him around by his dick."

"She doesn't like Jerry much."

"Not anymore. She doesn't like anybody much except herself."

"Okay. Now tell me what you want me to do about Jerry, straight out." He put a hand on the doorknob. "Otherwise I'm leaving."

"No, don't. Please."

He waited.

". . . Suppose I do know where he is," she said.

"I'm listening."

"Would you talk to him? If the right person . . . you know, somebody he could trust . . . I think that's all it would take."

"Why me? What about his father?"

"Jerry won't talk to him."

"Why not?"

"He's afraid to. Afraid his dad won't believe him."

"Does he know you came to see me?"

"No, it was my idea."

"What makes you think he'll talk to me, a stranger?"

"Maybe he won't. I don't know. I'm just desperate, that's all." She drew a shaky breath. "He has to talk to *somebody* before it's too late. He doesn't have any reason to be afraid of you. And he knows you got hurt by whoever's trying to make him look guilty."

"Does he have any idea who framed him or why?"

"No. I don't, either."

"You know that if I do talk to him and he won't go in voluntarily, I'm legally bound to give him up. I'd lose my license if I didn't."

"I know," she said in a small voice. "But it'd be a lot better that way than Kelso tracking him down." Her pale blue eyes appealed to him. "Will you, if I can get him to talk to you?"

In other circumstances Runyon might have turned her down. The assault and the concussion gave him a vested interest, but the quickest way for a private detective to lose his license was to get involved in a major felony investigation without permission. It just wasn't his business. But something else was his business—the job he'd come to Gray's Landing to do. He took a fierce pride in his work; if there was one thing he hated, it was to leave a job, any job, unfinished.

"All right," he said, "but it has to be in person, not on the phone." And if and when he did talk to Jerry Belsize, like it or not, he'd serve him with the subpoena at the same time.

8

TAMARA

So here she was. All set for another wild and crazy hip-hop Saturday night.

Livin' large, partyin' half the night and doing the nasty the other half. Down and dirty 'cause she was under thirty. Young and sweet and full of heat. Yeah, baby. You go, girl.

Except she wasn't going anywhere. Only hip-hop she'd be doing was sitting around on one hip or the other while she sucked down diet soda and then hopping up to go to the bathroom. Only nasty she'd be doing was in her fantasies, and she didn't even have enough of them right now to say hello to Mr. V. Only party she'd be going to was the pity party she was throwing for herself. Young and sweet and full of defeat.

She sighed. Didn't *have* to stay home on Saturday night. Could've called up Vonda or one of the other girlfriends and gone out roaming . . . except that Vonda and Lucille and Joleen all had steady men or other plans. Could've gone out by herself to one of the Mission or SoMa clubs, done the singles crawl, found some other lonely soul to spend the night with . . . except that she'd tried it before and the only guys she'd met were weird, like that stockbroker dude, Clement Rawls, with his blond wig hang-up.

Six thirty already. No place to go, and the only exercise she was getting was slap-talking herself for being a lump. She didn't feel like reading or vegging out in front of the tube or even listening to music. The only thing she did feel like was heading out to the nearest Golden Arches and stuffing herself on McGrease. Not that she would. Damn, no. Worked too hard to lose weight to start moving back into Fat City just because she was lonely and depressed and horny and about sixteen other things.

In spite of herself she wondered what Horace was doing tonight. Playing a gig with the Philadelphia Philharmonic . . . no, symphonies were dark during the summer. Out with Mary from Rochester, doing the town. Or home alone doing each other. Or maybe planning their big October wedding, making out the guest list. Tamara could just imagine him with his face all scrunched up the way it got when it was puzzling on something, saying, "What do you think, Mary, should we send my ex Tamara an invitation or not?"

Well, damn him and her, too. Second-chair cello, second

violinist—a couple of second-rate musicians who deserved each other and their second-rate lives in the City of Brotherly Love. She was well rid of that man. Sure she was. She knew it; everybody said so. So why did he keep popping up inside her head like a big black smiley jack-in-the-box?

Clue in, Tamara. You know why he keeps popping up. Takes time to get over somebody you thought was the love of your life. A lot more time than three months.

She hopped off the couch and went to pee again. World's smallest bladder. When she came out, she detoured into the kitchen and looked in the fridge. Bottle of sauvignon blanc, nice and cold. No. Only make her more depressed, and she'd feel worse in the morning. She looked at the cans of Diet Coke, made a face, and shut the door. Well? Gonna do what now?

Uh-huh.

Work.

Only thing she was likely to get her head into tonight. Most nights, for that matter. If it wasn't for the heavy agency caseload and the fact that she could do a lot of the Net searches and billing from home, somebody'd have to come in and scrape her off the wall.

Not that she minded the overtime. Thing was, she loved detective work, even the routine stuff. Never imagined she would, when she first went to work for Bill, after seeing Pop so tired from all the overtime he put in at the Redwood City PD and him drumming it into her and

Claudia's heads that one cop in the family was enough. Big career in the computer industry, that was what Tamara had mapped out for herself. But the detective business got into your blood after a while. Fascinating, for the most part. Stimulating—sometimes too stimulating. Partner in a growing concern, her own boss, and she made good money and eventually she'd make a lot more as the agency continued to expand.

Of course it had its downsides, same as police work. All the hours you had to put in, the sometimes boring routine, the kinds of people and situations you had to deal with . . .

Blink. New thought: The business not only sucks you in; it controls your life. Look at Bill, all those years running a one-man agency, a real workaholic loner before he met Kerry. Look at Jake, always on the move, still working 24-7 whenever he could, still a loner with his wife gone and his son not wanting anything to do with him. Look at her. Before she got into the game, she'd had a love life and a social life and she'd played hard and didn't worry about much and didn't have any hang-ups she couldn't deal with. Now here she was, no love life, no social life, a solitary working fool herself. Maybe there was something about the business that screwed up normal lives. Or maybe it was just that people like Bill and Jake and her were the ones who were attracted to it. Maybe she hadn't known herself as well as she'd thought; maybe underneath all the teenage grunge and cockiness and uptight racial bullshit there'd been a born workaholic loner inside her tubby body waiting to pop out.

Well, anyway, it was something to think about. Or not think about.

Okay. Work.

She went into the small second bedroom that Horace had used to practice cello compositions before the low-brow neighbors complained. The apartment was his before she moved in and it was still jammed with his memory and his scent. Damn hand-me-down, like his Toyota Camry. She'd keep the car a while longer, but no way was she going to renew the apartment lease come the end of October. She could afford a better neighborhood than the avenues fog belt, a bigger apartment, and besides, living well was the best revenge. Wasn't too early to start the hunt for a new place, see what was available in other parts of the city. Might as well start tomorrow. She didn't have anything better to do on another boring Sunday.

The stack of computer discs Bill had given her was on the secretary desk. They were from a PC, so she dragged her old laptop out of the closet and plugged it in and booted it up. The discs dated back four years, to the time of Nancy Mathias's marriage; each one had dates hand-printed on it, three months' worth of entries on each. She fed the first one in, waited for it to download. Nancy Mathias's diary. Dead woman's diary. She sighed. This ought to be fun, she thought.

It wasn't. All the entries were headed with the date and time they were written, which made the chronology easy to keep straight. But some were hard to decipher because the woman had been a sloppy typist and referred to people and places by their initials and didn't use any apostrophes. And at first the entries weren't all that interesting. Long descriptions of the Mathiases' honeymoon on Maui, places they went and things they did after they got back to Palo Alto. Shorthand comments on art and art galleries—painting in watercolors had been the woman's hobby—and somebody with the initials TQ whose impressionism she admired; on restaurants, plays, a ballet, weekend and holiday trips to some place called CV, wherever that was, probably a vacation home. Happy, chattery, lovey stuff. Almost every one had at least one reference to B—Brandon, her husband. Some of them were were embarrassing and annoying at the same time, like passages from a bad romance novel:

Every time I look at him, even now after three years together, my heart leaps. I never thought I was capable of such total devotional love for any man. I loved J but it was nothing like what I feel for B. I would walk through fire for him, I would lie curled at his feet like a dog if he asked me to. I have no pride, no mind of my own where he is concerned. I have no life without him.

No man was worth the slave attitude. What if she'd felt that way toward Horace? She'd be a basket case right now.

The references to the Mathiases' sex life were even worse:

B and I made love last night. Fabulous as always. He touches me so deeply in so many ways, with his hands and his mind and his soul. When he moves and swells inside me I feel as if Im soaring, as if there are two of me, one reveling in the moment, the other high above watching with tears of joy in her eyes.

Mercy!

The second disc was more of the same, only not quite as happy-sappy. End of honeymoon, back to reality. By the third disc, a few mild complaints started to creep in. He was critical of her opinions and her personal appearance. He demanded perfection and didn't like to be questioned about anything. They didn't make love as often; B was working long hours and he was so tired when he came home, poor baby. They didn't go out much anymore. They didn't go to CV together. B didn't like her sister, her friends, didn't want her to spend time with them away from home. Not that she minded, oh no. Whatever B wanted, B got.

It went on like that for more than three years, B tightening the reins until she was no longer seeing her sister or her friends, not going to CV by herself as she'd done a couple of times, not even going out of the house much anymore. Classic control-freak crap that got Tamara's blood heated up. But Nancy Mathias had bought into it with no more than an occasional whimper.

B made me cry again last night. I said something that displeased him, Im not even sure what it was, and he berated me mercilessly. Voice of ice, stare of ice. I look in his eyes and I see myself shriveled and cowering there and as always it frightens me to abject tears.

By the fourth year she wasn't much more than a good little robot, put away and waiting for the master to come home and turn on the juice. She didn't mention her painting or art galleries anymore. The entries were now one long dull, repetitive chronicle of what she ate and drank, what she read, the music she listened to, the little errands she ran. And B, naturally. Hardly a single entry without his initial in it.

Early this year, too late, she started to wake up. His hold on her was so tight she was feeling the pressure in physical ways—menstrual problems and intense migraine headaches. Every third or fourth entry was an expression of loneliness, bewilderment, frustration. Fear, too, that led her to question his love and commitment, if not hers. Tamara paid closer attention. Now she was getting to the kinds of things Bill had asked her to watch for.

Sometimes he looks at me as if Im nothing to him. Less than nothing, a piece of lint on his coat that he might brush off at any moment. It terrifies me. What if he decides hes had enough of me, brushes ME off? I cant conceive of living without him.

He doesnt hate me, he cant hate me, but his eyes last night, oh God, as if he wished I were dead. Did I imagine it? I must have. I know he loves me. He never says the words anymore, but I know he does. Hed never hurt me. He isnt a violent man, he has never touched me except with loving hands. How could he hate me?

So he'd never slapped her around, beat her up. Big deal. What the bastard *had* done was bad enough. In some ways, even worse.

B told me again how useless I am. How many times now? A hundred, a thousand? I cant stand it anymore. I had one of my worst migraines ever, the pain so bad I vomited and then had to lie down with a wet cloth over my eyes. He followed me, stood over me, berating and accusing the whole time. Does he really think I have migraines on purpose just to annoy him? I cant make him understand. I dont think he wants to understand.

Tamara scanned through a dozen similar entries. Woman'd had plenty to complain about, all right, but complain was all she'd done. Why? Why hadn't she walked out on the bastard, asked her sister or somebody for help?

Why did J have to die and leave me alone? I was happy with him, we had a wonderful life together; HE loved me as much as I loved him. If hed lived I would never have met B and sometimes now I wish I hadnt.

Well, there was the answer. Couldn't stand to be alone. Weak, dependent, and so beaten down and disillusioned all she could do was throw pity parties for herself.

A mid-February passage caught Tamara's attention:

B brought his new assistant home for dinner last night. He thinks the world of him, says he has a brilliant mind, and oh hes personable enough but there is something about him that puts me off. Im not sure what it is, other than a sly toadying quality and his physical appearance. Foolish to judge someone by his looks I suppose but you cant help an instinctive reaction. What kind of name is Drax anyway? Eastern European? It reminds me of Dracula. He reminds me of Dracula, the movie image, with his sharp teeth and odd eyes and leathery skin. I can imagine him in a swirling cape, his mouth all red with blood, and the image gives me chills. I haven't said anything to B about this, I dont dare, but I hope he wont invite him to the house again.

No more mention of Drax the vampire after that. The rest of the disc was the usual dull litany of books read and films watched on TV and doctors' and dentists' appointments and whines about B and one small desperate expression of hope on a morning after he decided it was time he got laid again.

The next entries that jumped out were on the last disc. First of these was dated August 23:

Yesterday
Yesterday I
Oh God I cant write about it I can barely think about it.
Its so its just too I just cant

Gap of two days. Then:

I told B last night. He has never shown his emotions but I could tell he was very very upset. I cried and told him how much I loved him and how sorry I was and he held me, so tender and loving the way he was in the beginning. It was all I could have hoped for.

The following week:

I was wrong, he doesnt give a damn about me! He didn't come to Ds yesterday as he promised, he made me go through it alone. His excuse was an important meeting he couldnt get out of. Important! A fucking meeting! What about me, I said, arent I important? Of course of course, he said, but he didnt mean it. He doesnt care. He never cared. I dont know what Im going to do.

The entries got shorter and shorter after that, with less information about what was going on in the woman's life. She got up, ate, took naps, watched TV, read, went to bed; B was there, B wasn't there. Flat, empty words that had to've come out of deep depression.

Then this one, five days before her death:

I cant go on alone. I could call C but I cant seem to bring myself to. God help me I still need B. I hate myself for needing him when I know now how he really feels about me and what a fool Ive been but I cant help myself. If I have to Ill go to M, Ill do something drastic to force B to be there for me. I CANT be alone now.

And two days before:

Another ugly fight with B last night. Another terrible headache, so bad I vomited and barely slept. Hes so cold, so unfeeling. He terrifies me when hes like that. His eyes, the way they look through me, it gives me chills. I think, no Im sure now, hes actually capable of doing me physical harm.

The final entry had been made on the day of her death. It was the shortest of any, just the date and time and two words in capital letters:

WHY ADHERE?

Tamara had been making notes all along; she made another, with a big question mark after it, then sat back and read through the list of direct quotes and her comments.

Not too much there, no real motive for Brandon the ass-hole to want to off his wife. But there sure were a lot of questions.

What had Nancy done that she couldn't write about, then confessed to him two days later?

What was it she'd had to go through without him at D's?

Did "D" stand for Drax the vampire?

Why was she so desperate those last couple of weeks?

Who was M and what was the "something drastic"?

What did that weird final entry mean?

Tamara stared at those last two words. *WHY ADHERE?* Why adhere to what? Her marriage? Life itself? Couldn't be a suicide note, could it? No, no way. Woman wanted to off herself, she'd swallow a bottle of pills or slash her wrists in the tub. One thing she'd never do is throw herself down a flight of stairs on the slim chance she'd break her neck.

Well, there was no use speculating without more facts. Bill had pounded that into her head enough times.

He terrifies me when hes like that. . . . I think, no Im sure now, hes actually capable of doing me physical harm.

Yeah. Enough meat here to justify an investigation. The hit she'd gotten from that entry and the others on the last disc was pretty strong. Call it intuition or whatever, some-thing had been wrong, bad wrong, in the woman's life, and her death sure could've been more than just a simple accident.

The laptop clock read 8:50. Not too late to call Bill and fill him in. If he didn't want to handle the investigation, she'd take it on herself.

9

JAKE RUNYON

The girl's voice on the phone was shrill, quivery. "He's gone! Jerry's *gone!*"

"Calm down; take a deep breath." Runyon waited for her to do that. "All right. What happened?"

"I don't know. I drove out here this morning, like we talked about, and he's not here. He didn't leave me a note or anything; he just . . . he's gone."

"He didn't say anything to you yesterday about going someplace else?"

"No, no. I don't understand why he'd leave here. He doesn't have anywhere else to go."

"Where are you?"

"At the camp. I'm on my cell."

"What camp?"

"Oh, right, you don't know. Old migrant workers'

camp on the Hammond farm. It hasn't been used for years."

"How do I get there?"

"It's about three miles from town. More east than south." She gave him directions, complicated enough so that he had to write them down.

"Stay there and wait for me. I'll make it as quick as I can."

Almost ten by his watch. He'd been up and dressed for three hours, sitting in the motel room for the last hour waiting for Sandra Parnell to call. There was enough of the headache left for him to be aware of it, but none of the aftereffects Dr. Yeng had warned him about. The swelling was down on his ear, and when he put on a new bandage from his first-aid kit the stitched wound on his temple hadn't shown any signs of infection. His appetite had been good this morning, even if the coffee shop food wasn't. He was ready to be out and on the move again.

It took him nearly half an hour to find the migrant workers' camp. Well out in the country, off a hardpan side road, surrounded by orchards and cattle graze, all flatland except for a couple of rocky hillocks in one of the fields, and no farm buildings in sight. Ghost camp. Dozen or so crumbling wood and cinder-block shacks, the single-room type, doorless, the glass long gone from their windows. Two small, rusted Quonset huts, also without doors or windows, and the remains of an ancient Airstream trailer. Built along a narrow stream, summer-dry now, shaded by willows and cottonwoods and overgrown with weeds, dead grass, clumps of manzanita. The sun, already hot in the eastern sky, gave it all the look of a mass of tinder lighted by a match flame.

Sandra Parnell's Chrysler was drawn in under one of the willows, so that it couldn't be seen until you came in off the side road; rows of fruit trees hid the camp from the county blacktop beyond. She was waiting beside the car, smoking. She dropped the butt and ground it out quickly under the heel of her flip-flop as he pulled up nearby.

The gathering heat folded around him when he got out. The girl hurried over, bringing the faint smell of marijuana along with her. The joint hadn't been her first; the glaze on her eyes told him that. Not cheap, just young and stupid. However many she'd smoked, they'd taken the edge off her anxiety. She stood slack shouldered, the way people do when there has been an easing of tension.

"I looked everywhere," she said. "There's just no sign of him or his car."

"Where was he holed up? One of the shacks?"

"No, the trailer."

The weeds and dry grass were littered with discarded belongings, splintered doors, bent sheet-metal panels, a rusted set of box springs. Runyon picked his way around and through them to the Airstream skeleton. Its door was shut. When he pulled it open, trapped heat heavy with the stink of dust and decay, fast food and marijuana, emptied out at him. He put his head inside, then the rest of his body, breathing through his mouth.

Sunlight slanting in through one of the broken windows showed him a gutted interior, the floor overlain with debris, rodent turds, a dozen or so roach butts smoked down to nubbins. Empty except for an old, worn sleeping bag and the leavings of a recent McDonald's meal. Both brought by the girl, probably.

He kicked around in there for a minute or so. The only other thing that caught his eye was a torn piece of colored paper, squared off on two sides. He picked it up. Some kind of label, blank and glue-smooth on one side. A caked, sticky blob adhered to the colored side, obscuring a design; all he could make out was what looked like a tree and rubbed and smeared lettering that seemed to be part of a word or name: *RipeO*. It didn't look as though it had been there long. Brought in on the bottom of a shoe, maybe, and pulled or scraped off.

He took it outside with him, showed it to Sandra. "This mean anything to you?"

She blinked at it. "No. What is it?"

"Probably nothing." But he pocketed it anyway. "What kind of car does Jerry drive?" he asked her.

"'Fifty-seven Impala. Dark blue, tuck-and-roll upholstery."

"Easy to spot."

"Yes. Why would he go driving around?"

Not thinking straight. Running scared. Or maybe he had unfinished business somewhere. "Last time you saw him was when?"

"Yesterday afternoon. About five."

"He was holed up here since Friday night?"

"Yes."

"Where was he all that day? Why didn't he go home when he was supposed to?"

Her glazed eyes shifted away from his. "I don't know."

"Sure you do. Last night you said you couldn't tell me. That was last night; this is today. Where was he on Friday?"

"It . . . doesn't have anything to do with what happened to Manuel. Or the fires or any of that."

"Where was he, Sandra?"

She chewed her lip, making up her mind whether or not to answer. "He . . . oh, all right. He was in Lost Bar."

"Where's that?"

"Mountains up by Weaverville."

"Doing what?"

"Buying some grass. There's a guy has a pot farm up there."

"How big a buy?"

"You won't tell anybody about this, will you?"

"Not if I don't have to. Answer the question. How big a buy?"

"Half a kilo."

"For resale?"

"No! Just for, you know, me and a few friends."

"Where did he get the money?"

"Saved some from his job. And I gave him some."

"Anybody else?"

"Uh . . . Bob Varley."

"Who's he?"

"Just a guy Jerry hangs out with. He works at the Gasco station out by the freeway."

"Big kid, red hair, not too bright?"

"Yeah, that's Bob."

"The owner of this pot farm—what's his name?"

"Gus something. Funny last name. German, I think."

"How well does Jerry know him?"

"Just to buy grass from, that's all."

"How much grass? How often?"

"Every few months, whenever we run out." She ran her tongue over her lips again. "We're not druggies," she said defensively. "We don't get high that often, just sometimes on weekends, you know?"

"You're stoned now," Runyon said.

"Oh God, I couldn't help it. I'm so scared . . . I needed something . . . You won't tell anybody?"

"Show me where Jerry had his car hidden."

She led him back into the woods along the creek bank. The dry grass was mashed down in there in parallel tracks. Manzanita and scrub grew thickly, some of the branches and smaller bushes twisted and broken. Runyon prowled the area, hunting for foreign objects. All he found was a couple of rusted tin cans and a scatter of used condoms.

He asked, "Did you come out here with him on Friday night?"

"No."

"But you saw him that night. Where? What time?"

"At my house—my folks were out. After ten, after he got back from Lost Bar."

"Why was he so late getting back?"

"He had some trouble up there."

"What kind of kind of trouble? With Gus?"

"No, something with his car. He had to get it fixed at the garage."

Runyon asked, "Why did he go to you instead of home?"

"We were supposed to meet at five and he knew I'd be worried."

"So were his parents. He could've called them. Or you."

"He doesn't have a cell. He doesn't like to talk on the phone."

"But it was all right that his parents were worried."

"I don't know, I guess he just didn't think . . ."

"You tell him what happened at the farm?"

She nodded. "If he'd got to my house five minutes earlier, Kelso would've caught him."

"Is that how you found out, from Kelso?"

"Yeah. He came around looking for Jerry. Made it real plain he thought Jerry was guilty."

"So Jerry panicked and decided to hide out here. For how long?"

"He wasn't thinking that far ahead. He just didn't want to be arrested for something he didn't do. And this was the only place he could think of where nobody'd think to look—" She broke off, her body stiffening, her head craned forward. "Shit! Somebody's coming!"

Runyon heard the engine sound. Through the rows of fruit trees he had glimpses of the car barreling down the side road at a high rate of speed. Sunlight glinted off the row of unlit flashers across its roof as it swerved in toward the camp, outlined the sheriff's department insignia on the side door.

"Kelso, it's Kelso!" The girl clutched at Runyon's arm; her nails were as sharp as claws. "What're we going to do?"

"Nothing. You just be quiet, let me do the talking."

"But he—"

"Quiet, I said."

He took her arm, steered her back into the camp. The cruiser bucked to a stop behind Runyon's Ford. Kelso was alone; he came out fast, unsheathing his weapon, moving ahead with it in his hand. Big, tough, his face flushed, his stride hard as if he were stomping something with each step. A cowboy, all right. Runyon stopped himself and Sandra next to one of the shacks, let Kelso come to them.

"What the devil are you doing here, Runyon?"

"Same thing you are. Looking for Jerry Belsize."

"Is that so? Where is he?"

"Gone."

"Gone? Gone where?" Then, to the girl, "Where is he, Sandy?"

She was coming down off her high; she stood tense and frightened. "I don't know. I swear I don't."

"But you knew he was here. Knew it when I talked to you Friday night."

"No—"

"Yes, by God." Kelso made another visual sweep of the area, then jammed his weapon back into its holster. His fury was a tangible thing; you could see it in the play of muscles in his face, the blade-edge cords in his neck. "You, Runyon. How'd you know to come out here?"

"Sandra asked me to come."

"Oh, she did? What for?"

"Talk to Jerry, try to convince him to come in voluntarily."

Kelso didn't like that. "Why you?"

"Look at her. She's terrified of you."

"She has good reason to be, harboring a fugitive."

"That's not exactly right," Runyon said mildly. "Belsize isn't a fugitive; he's only wanted for questioning. Unless some new evidence has turned up to change his status."

Kelso didn't respond. He glared at the girl. "You shouldn't have lied to me," he said.

"I'm sorry, Mr. Kelso, honest, but Jerry didn't set those fires, he didn't kill anybody, he—"

"He's guilty as sin."

Runyon said, "Either way, guilty or innocent, he's just as afraid of you as she is."

"What do you know about it? You don't know squat."

"If you say so."

"I say so. You should've reported it when the girl told you about this place. Did your duty instead of hotfooting it out here, sticking your nose in where it doesn't belong."

"Maybe so."

"No maybes about it. I ought to report *you* for with-holding information in a criminal case."

"Go ahead. But I told you why I came. If Jerry hadn't listened to me, I'd've taken him to Rinniak anyway."

"That's what you say."

"It's the truth. Ask Sandra."

"That's right," she said. "He told me that before he—"

"Shut up, girl. You speak when you're spoken to. I haven't made up my mind what I'm going to do about you yet."

Runyon said, "Can I ask you a question, Deputy?"

"I don't have to answer questions from you."

"How'd *you* know to come out here?"

There was a heavy silence before the deputy said, clipping the words, "Anonymous phone call."

Sandra sucked in her breath. "Oh God. Was it a man or a woman?"

"What difference does that make?"

"It's a reasonable question," Runyon said.

"Disguised voice, not that it's any more your business than hers."

He returned the deputy's hard stare without blinking. Before long the stare moved back to the girl. She shrank under it, looking down and away. The acrid marijuana fumes had dissipated, but her eyes still had the glaze. Kelso didn't seem to notice. Too wrapped up in his anger and frustration.

"Stay here, both of you," he said finally. "Don't go

anywhere." He hitched up his Sam Browne belt, swung away from them to prowl the camp.

When he was out of earshot, Runyon said to the girl, "Did you tell anybody besides me about Jerry being here?"

"No. Nobody, I swear."

"How about Friday night? Were you alone when Jerry showed up?"

She nodded. "He was sure nobody followed him. How could anyone else have known?"

Question begging an answer. He said, "You have any more pot on you or in your car?"

"Pot?" She whispered it, glancing furtively toward where Kelso was poking around the rusted trailer. "No."

"If you do and he finds it, he'll make it hard on you."

"I know. But I don't have any more."

"If you're smart, you'll keep it that way."

Kelso vanished inside the trailer. He didn't stay long. When he came out he made straight to where Runyon and the girl waited, a tight little satisfied smile on his mouth. "Marijuana butts in there, plenty of them. Drugs as well as arson and murder."

Runyon said nothing. Neither did Sandra.

"Now he's not just wanted for questioning," Kelso said. "Now he's wanted for possession and probable sale of marijuana."

"Jerry never sold any grass!"

The deputy withered her with another of his stares.

"You know where he went, girl, you'd better tell me right now."

"I don't, I swear to God."

"You'd better pray for His mercy if you're lying to me."

Runyon said, "Why don't you give her a break, Kelso?"

"Don't try to tell me my business." The deputy's voice held a belligerent dare. "I don't like it. I don't like you. Keep sticking your oar in, I'll lay an obstruction charge on you. You hear?"

"I hear."

"All right then. Sandra, you get in your car and follow me back to town. Stay right behind me all the way."

"Oh shit, Mr. Kelso, you're not arresting me?"

"Watch your mouth. I don't stand for foul language from you or any other kid. You just do what I tell you."

"But I don't *know* anything!"

"Get in your car. Now."

The girl threw Runyon an anguished look of appeal. He took it stoically; there was nothing he could do. In spite of the heat, she folded her arms across her breasts as if she were suddenly chilled, slunk away to the Chrysler.

Kelso poked a finger in Runyon's direction, stopping it just short of his chest. "I'll be seeing you again. Count on it."

Runyon didn't trust himself to respond.

He stood watching Kelso back his cruiser around, Sandra maneuver her Chrysler into position behind it. She glanced over at him again just before they pulled out, her face pale and sweat beaded. He gave her a thumbs-up gesture that she didn't acknowledge. She had the fearful look of a prisoner awaiting sentence by a hanging judge.

10

Sunday mornings are quiet times in my household. We're not churchgoers, but that doesn't mean, no matter what the hard-core religious right would have you believe, that we lack spirituality or traditional family values. Organized religion is fine for some people; for others it's restrictive and unnecessary. There's a wryly funny and sage comment in an Agatha Christie film I saw once that pretty much sums up my position, and Kerry's. One of the characters in the film tells Miss Marple that an odd young man of her acquaintance was once arrested for exposing himself in St. Paul's Cathedral. After a thoughtful moment, Miss Marple replies, "Well, we all worship in our own way."

I got up first and cooked breakfast, and Emily and I spent some quality time together, talking about this and that, things that matter to eleven-year-old girls and their doting adoptive fathers, while Kerry had her breakfast in bed and read everything in the Sunday paper except the ads. She doesn't share my anti-news philosophy. Her attitude is the generally accepted one that the better informed you are, the better able you are to cope. We've had any number of discussions on the subject, my stance being the generally unaccepted one that the better informed you are, the more frustrated and crazy you're liable to become. Unless you're a dedicated activist, there's damn little you can do about such matters as global terrorism, indefensible wars on foreign soil and escalating body counts, widespread political corruption, drug-related gang violence, and all the other insanities that make up the daily news. Cast your vote, contribute to appropriate causes, raise your public voice now and then, try to make a difference in small, work-related ways, and hope for the best—that's about it. You don't need daily details of barbarism and polarized op-ed columns and strings of depressing statistics to do any of those things. One man's opinion. We all worship in our own way and we all get through the best way we can.

Emily and I cleaned up the kitchen, after which she went into her room to commune with her iPod and I shut myself inside Kerry's office to find out if Celeste Ogden was available. After Tamara's call last night, and her report on what she'd found in Nancy Mathias's diary, I agreed that we were justified in pursuing an investigation. Up to a point. Cases like this, as I'd tried to tell Mrs. Ogden on Friday, are tricky. Unless you turn up incontrovertible evidence that a crime has been committed, there's only so much you can do. We'd take it one step at a time, see what developed. If nothing did, we'd bow out whether the client liked it or not.

Might as well notify her right away. Sundays are quiet days, family days, but there's no hard-and-fast rule that says you can't sneak in a little business now and then.

Celeste Ogden answered the phone herself. She wasn't surprised to hear from me on a Sunday morning, and all she said when I told her we were going ahead was, "Now you understand what kind of man he is, why I believe he was responsible for Nancy's death." She hadn't expected anything less from me.

"I understand why you have suspicions, yes."

"He killed her," she said. "Whether it was his hand that pushed her down those stairs or not."

"If he did it may or may not be provable, no matter what our investigation turns up. There's nothing specific among her effects or in her diary to suggest foul play, or even a motive for foul play."

"You're capable of reading between the lines, just as I am."

I didn't see any purpose in telling her that I hadn't gone through the diary discs myself. I said, "A few questions, Mrs. Ogden."

"Of course."

I consulted the notes I'd made during Tamara's call. "The diary entry dated August 23. Your sister was so upset about something she couldn't write about it. Any idea what it was?"

"No. Something to do with him, no doubt."

"Two days later she wrote that she told her husband about it. An affair or brief sexual encounter, possibly?"

"Nancy? Lord, no. Never."

"Why so positive?"

"Her morals would never have allowed an extramarital affair. My sister was the most moral person I've ever known. She was still a virgin, and proud of the fact, when she married John Ring at age twenty-four."

I took the opinion with a few grains of salt. People change as they get older; so do their morals. If Nancy Mathias's closed-off life and coldly controlling husband had become intolerable enough, it was entirely possible that she'd turned to another man for comfort and understanding.

"What do you think she was afraid to go through alone at D's?"

"I don't know. Some sort of crisis, obviously. Nancy was very dependent—I believe I told you that. She couldn't bear to be alone, particularly during any sort of crisis. When John, her first husband, died she surrounded herself with people for weeks afterward."

"Do you know her husband's assistant, the man named Drax?"

"Anthony Drax. I met him at the funeral."

"What do you think of him?"

"He's a perfect complement to his employer. Brilliant,

charming, ambitious, and bereft of any decent human feelings. No doubt that's why he was hired."

"'D' might stand for Drax," I said.

"I don't see how it could. Nancy didn't care for the man any more than I did. She made that plain enough."

"Do any of her friends or acquaintances have names that start with 'D'?"

"Not that I know of."

"Her reference to doing something drastic," I said. "Was she capable of divorcing Mathias?"

"If she were driven to it. Divorce or legal separation— yes, that's possible. She made an appointment with her attorney three days before her death, but she didn't keep it. I know because I called him."

"She didn't tell him what she wanted to see him about?"

"Apparently not. He said she sounded upset on the phone."

"You told me there was no prenuptial agreement. Did Nancy keep any assets in her own name when she and Mathias were married, assets he would've lost out on in a community property divorce?"

"John's stocks and bonds. She felt that the portfolio should remain in her name, in honor of his memory."

"Did Mathias object?"

"She said he didn't."

"How much does the portfolio amount to?"

"I don't know exactly. Several hundred thousand dollars."

"Are any of the bonds the bearer type?"

"Yes. I thought of that, too."

Motive there, if Mathias needed a large sum of money in a hurry and had access to those bearer bonds and had been cashing them on the sly.

She said, "There are other possibilities besides financial gain, you know. A divorce or separation would have been an embarrassment to him, a blow to his ego. And a professional distraction."

"People don't commit murder because they're embarrassed or distracted."

"Don't they? You don't know him as I do. That man is capable of anything to further his own ends."

I let that pass. "One of the things that stands out among your sister's records is the ten-thousand-dollar check to T. R. Quentin. Do you know who that is?"

"An artist she admired, evidently. Someone I've never met."

"So the check could be for the purchase of some of his paintings."

"It could be, I suppose."

"Was your sister in the habit of spending large sums on artworks?"

"She bought paintings now and then—she loved art, even though she had little enough talent herself—but not at inflated prices."

"Ten thousand is a lot of money for a woman in distress to spend on paintings."

"Not necessarily. Nancy was capable of extravagance when she was upset or depressed. After John died, she spent thousands on new furniture—an attempt to deflect her grief."

"Have you talked to T. R. Quentin?"

"No. Nor should you bother. He's not the person you need to concern yourself with."

Don't tell me how to conduct an investigation, lady, I thought. But I didn't say it. She wasn't somebody you could argue with, and she was hurting underneath all that quiet rage and hatred; why make the professional relationship any more difficult for either of us?

Before I ended the call I asked her for the name and address of her sister's attorney and for the address of the cleaning woman, Philomena Ruiz.

When I opened the office door, Kerry was just coming out of the bedroom in her robe and slippers, a page from the pink section of the Sunday paper in one hand. "There you are," she said. "What do you think I found in the Events listing?"

"What?"

"The Brookline Gallery downtown is sponsoring a show by a local artist that just opened yesterday. Guess who the artist is."

"T. R. Quentin?"

"None other."

"Brookline's one of the better galleries, isn't it? He must be pretty well-known."

"She," Kerry said. "T.R. stands for Theodora Rose, it says here."

"Well, there goes an idea."

"That Nancy Mathias and T. R. Quentin were having an affair and the ten-thousand-dollar check was a loan or a blackmail payoff?"

I raised an eyebrow. "You've been hanging around me too long. Your mind is getting to be as devious as mine."

"It's still a possibility, if Theodora Rose is a lesbian and Nancy was bisexual."

"Even more devious than mine. I doubt it. But then you never know."

"I wonder," Kerry said, "if artists spend their Sundays at galleries where their show has just opened."

"What, you think I should I go down to the Brookline today?"

"Why don't we both go? Emily, too. We haven't been to an art gallery in quite a while."

"All right with me, if you're sure that's how you want to spend a Sunday afternoon."

"What I want," she said, "and what I need, is to start doing the things I enjoy, feeling normal again."

Amen to that.

The Brookline Gallery, Purveyors of Fine Art, was on Post Street, off Union Square. Fronting the sidewalk was a broad bay window, inside of which a single large oil painting was displayed on an easel. In the window itself, a placard lettered in gilt-edged black: **PRESENTING THE IMPRESSIONIST VISIONS OF T. R. QUENTIN.**

"That's one of her visions in the window," Kerry said.

I looked at it before we went inside. Riotous swirls and whorls and globs and blobs of rainbow colors—yellow, red, blue, purple dominating—intermingled with solid black geometric designs of varying sizes. A gold plaque on the base of the frame gave its title as *Searches*. It didn't do much for me; if I looked at it too long and in the wrong frame of mind I'd probably want to retitle it *Searches and Seizures*.

Emily said, "I like it. Don't you, Mom?"

"Yes, it's interesting."

"Dad?"

"Personally I prefer pulp covers."

Kerry said, "Lowbrow," and we went on inside.

The Brookline's interior was set up along the lines of a museum. One large room, two smaller ones, lots of open space, long walls and short ells built in and created by movable partitions, benches for restful viewing of the art-works on display. There must have been more than fifty paintings of varying sizes—acrylic, oil, watercolor—plus a handful of tapestries. At the entrance to one of the smaller rooms, a duplicate of the window placard was propped on an easel to let you know that that was where the Quentin pieces were exhibited. Kerry and I went in there. Something else caught Emily's eye and she went scooting off by herself to check it out. In some ways she was your typical eleven-year-old; in others she was a full-fledged adult. Most kids would have balked at a Sunday afternoon visit to an art galley. Emily relished it.

The Quentin room was occupied by two women, one elderly and overly dressed, the other younger and fashionably attired. Customer and gallery employee, from the snatches of conversation I overheard. Kerry and I took a look at the dozen or so paintings in there. All were similar to the one in the front window, some with broader, sweeping brushstrokes, others done in colors that were more or less bright. Each had varying numbers of solid black squares, rectangles, oblongs, triangles, trapezoids. On the bottom corners of their frames small, discreetly placed price tags said that they could be had for from $750 for the smallest to $5,000 for the largest. Kerry didn't think the prices were out of line, given the value placed on quality contemporary art these days. Nice money if you could get it. Or if you had it to spend.

"Kandinsky," she said.

"How's that?"

"Her major influence. Wassily Kandinsky, one of the Blue Riders."

"If you say so."

"The Blue Riders were a group of artists in Munich in the early twentieth century. Specializing in nonobjective, free-form abstracts."

I nodded and said, "Uh-huh," and the two women finished their conversation and the younger one came over to where we were.

"Aren't these wonderful?" she said, smiling. "Ms. Quentin is such a talented artist. We feel privileged to have her exhibiting with us."

"Wonderful," I agreed. "Very colorful. Would Ms. Quentin happen to be here today, by any chance?"

"As a matter of fact, she is. In the office with a customer at the moment. Would you like a word with her?"

"Whenever it's convenient."

"Please wait. She should be available shortly."

We waited about five minutes. The woman who came bustling in alone was on the backside of forty, all smiles and rouged cheeks, wearing an outfit as multihued as her paintings; slim and trim and poised in her movements, projecting an air of cheerful self-confidence. The only jarring note was dark red hair combed or uncombed, take your pick, in spiky juts and tangles. Kerry told me later that the haircut was fashionable among young people, both men and women, these days. My response to that was, "Why?"

We introduced ourselves. Were Kerry and I prospective buyers? No, we weren't. That put a crimp in her smile, and when I told her I was employed by Nancy Mathias's sister, it morphed all the way into a sad downturn. She didn't ask what I did for Celeste Ogden and I didn't volunteer the information. She said, "I was so sorry to read about Mrs. Mathias's death. A terrible tragedy."

Mrs. Mathias, not Nancy. "You didn't know her well?"

"No, hardly at all. I wish I had."

"I understand she bought some of your paintings shortly before her accident."

"Actually, no, she didn't."

"But she did pay you a large sum of money. Ten thousand dollars."

"'Pay' isn't the right word. It was a gift, you see."

"Oh? Pretty substantial gift."

T. R. Quentin's eyes brightened; the smile threatened to reestablish itself. "It absolutely floored me. It was like . . . I don't know, winning a lottery prize. Manna from heaven."

"How did it come about?"

"She called me one day at my studio. Out of the blue. Said she was a great admirer of my work and if we could meet, I'd find it well worth my time. Naturally I thought she intended to buy one of my paintings. So I invited her to come to the studio."

"You'd never had any contact with her before?"

"None. She was a complete stranger."

"Did she take you up on the invitation?"

"The following afternoon. She didn't stay long, not more than twenty minutes. She had another appointment in the city, she said."

"She happen to mention who the appointment was with?"

"No, she didn't."

"And she only stayed twenty minutes?"

"About that. We had coffee; she looked at my finished work; she asked a few discreet questions about my financial situation and my future goals. And then she wrote out that check. Well, I nearly fainted when I saw the amount. Every struggling artist dreams of a patron like Mrs. Mathias, but to have one actually appear, all of a sudden like that . . . well, I'm still in the pinch-me stage."

"Did you ask her why she was giving you such a large amount?"

"Of course. She said it was the least she could do to help an artist who was going to be famous someday." Color came into the woman's cheeks, all but making the spots of rouge disappear, but it wasn't the modest or humble type of blush. Nancy Mathias was not the only one who believed the "famous" prediction. "I offered to let her take any of my finished paintings she liked, more than one, but she refused. She simply shook my hand and wished me good fortune and walked out of my life as suddenly as she came into it."

"Why did she refuse the offer, if she liked your work so much?"

"I don't know. All she said was that she wouldn't be able to enjoy the paintings."

"Those her exact words?"

"I think it was something like, 'I won't be able to enjoy them where I'm going. Let others have the pleasure and the rewards.'"

"She didn't indicate where it was she'd be going?"

"No, she didn't. I thought it might be that she was planning to move to another state or another country—you know, change and downsize her life. But that's just my impression."

"How did she seem to you that day?"

"Seem? I'm not sure what you mean."

"Her demeanor, her state of mind. Was she happy, sad?"

"Well . . . not happy. And not exactly sad. Preoccupied, as if she had other things weighing on her mind."

"And you never saw her again?"

"No. I tried to call her the next day to thank her again—her phone number was on the check—but her machine picked up. I left a message, but she didn't return the call. So naturally I didn't bother her again."

Naturally. She'd gotten all the golden eggs out of the goose that she was going to and had the intellect to know when to back off. Or maybe I was just being cynical. Give her the benefit of the doubt.

Kerry and I collected Emily and went on out to Post Street. "I saw a really cool painting in there," the kid said. "It looks like a photograph of a stained-glass window, the kind with light shining through it, but it's not; it was done with oils. It'd look great on our living room wall."

"Would it?" Kerry said. "How much is it?"

"Only twenty-five hundred dollars."

Only twenty-five hundred. Only. If my two ladies had their way, we'd be in hock up to our eyebrows and I'd be confronted with modern culture every time I walked into the condo. My idea of eye candy in the home? Pulp magazines and their lurid four-color covers, any day.

11

JAKE RUNYON

He had no good reason to make a two-hundred-mile round-trip drive to the Trinity Alps. No business doing it with a concussion that had already cost him a night in the hospital. If he'd sat down and thought it over carefully, he might have talked himself out of it. But he didn't. He didn't feel like going back to the motel in Gray's Landing, hanging around there sweltering all day; he needed to be on the move. And why drive around aimlessly, going nowhere, when you had a specific place to check out?

Alone at the migrant camp, he got out his California map and pinpointed Lost Bar. It was a flyspeck on Highway 3, southeast of Weaverville, in the mountains some sixty miles east of Redding. Then, without thinking any more about it, he started driving.

Due north on Highway 5, then northwest from Redding

on 299 and into the Trinity Alps. Scenic route. Twisty road, thick forest land, views of snow-crested peaks and a big lake from Buckhorn Summit, the winding trail of the Trinity River. Gold Rush country. The fever had struck up here, too, at about the same time as it had down at Sutter's Mill: hard-rock miners, gold dredgers. Hillsides and back-waters were probably still honeycombed with hundred-and-fifty-year-old diggings. It was cooler at the higher elevations, a relief from the sticky heat of the valley; the air felt good in his lungs, streaming in against his face. The dull headache all but disappeared. More or less back to normal.

At a wide spot called Douglas City, a few miles below Weaverville, Highway 3 branched off to the southeast—a rougher county road that jiggled its way into the lower reaches of the Shasta-Trinity National Forest. Lost Bar lay in a small valley below Hayfork Summit, along the bank of Hayford Creek. Hayfork, Hayford—go figure the dif-ference. Another wide spot. Maybe a dozen buildings, two-thirds of them old frame houses and newer mobile homes flanked by meadows and trees. Grocery store, Lost Bar Saloon, Brody's Garage, and a pair of hollowed-out, collapsing ruins—one of redwood with BLACKSMITH burned into an ancient chain-hung sign, the other a smaller brick-and-mortar structure that bore the barely discernible words ASSAY OFFICE above its gaping entrance.

Runyon turned onto the apron in front of Brody's Garage, stopped short of the single gas pump. The place was open; inside the big main door, a man in greasy over-alls was working on something that looked like a tractor.

The mechanic straightened and swung around, wiping his hands on a rag even greasier than his overalls, as Runyon approached. Late forties, early fifties, thin and bald except for a fringe of stringy brown hair above the ears. Eyes that jumped and darted this way and that, as if he were afflicted with some sort of optical anomaly.

"Didn't expect to find you open on a Sunday," Runyon said.

"We're always open. Got to be, up here."

"Are you Mr. Brody?"

"Sam Brody, that's right. What'll it be? Gas, oil?"

"Information."

"About what?"

"My son. Jerry. He was up this way last Friday, had some trouble with his car, and got it fixed here. Called his mother about it, said he'd be home yesterday. But he didn't show up."

The jumpy eyes paused and held for three or four beats. "Is that right?"

"He's a flaky kid. Disappears every now and then, doing Christ knows what twenty-two-year-old kids do these days. But his mother worries. She sent me out to hunt for him."

"Last Friday?" Brody said. "What kind of car he drive?"

"'Fifty-seven Chevy Impala. Dark blue. Hot stuff."

"Nope."

"Nope?"

"I'd remember a car like that. Never saw it, last Friday or any other time."

"Were you here all day Friday?"

"All day."

"That's funny," Runyon said. "Jerry told his mother he was having the car fixed at the garage in Lost Bar. There another garage around here?"

"Nope. Next closest is in Hayfork. Maybe he meant Hayfork."

"He usually says what he means."

"Can't help you then."

Runyon said, "I wonder if he saw Gus."

The eyes stopped darting again. Brody's face flattened out and went blank, like a shutter snapping into place across a murky window. "Gus who?"

"Local guy Jerry came here to see."

"Don't know him."

"You sure? German, owns property nearby?"

"Sorry," Brody said. "I got to finish my work." He started away, paused long enough to glance back and say, "Kids, like you said. Your boy'll turn up okay," and then let the garage swallow him again.

Runyon U-turned the Ford across the highway to park in front of the Lost Bar General Store. The interior was gloomy, faintly dank, dominated by the smells of deli meats and the creosote they used on the buckled wooden floor. Close-packed shelves, one checkout stand with a fat woman in her forties behind it, one customer buying a loaf of bread and a six-pack of Coors. Runyon wandered to the cold cases in back, picked out a bottle of Lipton iced tea, brought it back up front. The other customer was gone by then. He paid for the tea before he asked his questions. Different approach this time, a reverse of the one he'd taken with Brody.

"I'm looking for a German fellow named Gus," he said, "owns property in the area. Can you tell me how to get to his place?"

"How come?"

"How come what?"

"How come you want Gus Mayerhof?"

"Private business matter."

"On a Sunday?"

"Good as any other day."

"Not if you're not expected."

"I'm not, but I think he'll want to see me. In fact, I'm sure he will."

"He's got a dog, Gus has. Mean bugger of a pit bull, tear your throat out if he gives it the right command. Keeps it because he don't like strangers coming around unannounced."

"Let me have his phone number and I'll call him first."

"He don't have a phone."

"Just directions, then. I'll take my chances with the pit bull."

The fat woman eyed his bandage. "What happened to your head?"

"A little accident. Nothing serious."

"Be real serious if you tangle with that dog."

He said nothing, watching her, waiting.

"You want a lot for a bottle of iced tea," she said.

He found a five-dollar bill and laid it on the counter. She looked it for maybe five seconds, looked up at him again with expectant, greedy eyes.

He said, "Five's all it's worth," and started to pick up the bill.

Her sausage fingers stopped him.

"Well, it's your hide, mister," she said. "Half a mile west there's a road cuts off into the wilderness. Peters out into a dirt track after about four miles. Another mile or so, there's a gate with a No Trespassing sign on it."

He let her make the five disappear before he said, "Couple more questions before I go. Were you working last Friday?"

"Every damn day except Monday."

"You happen to see a husky kid in his early twenties, driving a dark blue 'fifty-seven Impala?"

"I don't know nothing about cars."

"You couldn't miss this one. Might've been over at Brody's part of the day."

"Didn't notice if it was."

"How about yesterday or today? Any young guys come in, strangers?"

"We don't get too many strangers in here, even in summer. Who's this kid, anyway?"

Runyon said, "Thanks for your help," and left her excavating an ear canal with the tip of her little finger.

The Lost Bar Saloon was a squarish log building incongruously topped with a huge satellite dish that loomed up like one of the radar scanners at the SRI complex. The reason for the dish was apparent when Runyon walked in. The bartender and three beer drinkers, two male and one female, were all watching a pro football game on a wide-screen TV, the volume turned up so high you couldn't hold a conversation without half-shouting. Their interest in him was brief, vanished altogether when he asked his questions. Indifferent responses void of information. None of them had seen a dark blue '57 Impala in the vicinity recently, or would own up to it if they had.

He closed himself inside the Ford again and rolled out of Lost Bar, following the fat woman's directions. The wilderness road was a bent and crimped tunnel bored through thick stands of pine, alternately climbing and dropping, bypassing the crumbling hillside remains of a sluice mine. The going got rougher after pitted asphalt gave way to potholed hardpan; he had to drive at a crawl to avoid damage to the tires and undercarriage. The jouncing restarted the ache in his head. He clamped his teeth together and slowed down even more.

After a mile and two-tenths by the odometer, he rounded a curve and there was the gated entrance to Gus Mayerhof's property. The gate and the barbed-wire fencing strung out on both sides were plastered with **No Trespassing** signs, all of them handmade. If the gate had been shut and locked, he'd have had to consider whether or not to go in on foot; but it stood open, like an invitation. The access road was a scar on the hillside, heavily furrowed by the erosion of rain and winter snows, climbing up through deep woods. It crested after five hundred yards or so, and the trees thinned; and as he started down on the other side he was looking at a home place like none he'd seen before.

It wasn't a house or a cabin or a shack; it was a patchwork, spare-parts thing made of wood and brick and tarpaper and sheet metal, sprawling and sagging and jutting at odd angles among tall lodgepole pines. Smoke curled from a stovepipe chimney in one corner of an uneven A-frame roof. A lean-to to one side sheltered a newish Dodge pickup. The front and side yards were littered with the corpses and skeletons of two trucks, a passenger car, a wood stove, an old-fashioned icebox, dozens of less recognizable items.

There was no front porch, just a pair of concrete steps built into a foundation slab below the door. The man standing on the bottom step didn't move as Runyon drove into the yard. Bearded and shaggy-haired, big-bellied in a khaki shirt and military camouflage pants, he had a shotgun slung over one arm and a chain leash tight-wrapped in the other hand. The pit bull, black and vicious looking, strained at the other end of the chain, barking furiously, foamy drool flying from its jowls. There was no expression on the man's blocky face. The way he stood, flat-footed, motionless, made him seem even bigger than he was.

He remained motionless until Runyon parked at a slant behind one of the rusted-out wrecks. Then he came forward in a long, stiff-backed stride, like a giant stick man, to within a dozen yards of the Ford. When he stopped again he jerked once on the chain and the pit bull immediately quit barking, sat on its haunches, and stared at Runyon with red-eyed malevolence.

"I don't know you," in a big bass rumble. "Stay where you are, you know what's good for you."

"Gus Mayerhof?"

"Got eyes, ain't you? Know how to read signs?"

"Your gate was open."

"You better have a goddamn good reason for driving through it."

"I'm looking for a kid named Jerry Belsize. Lives down in the valley—Gray's Landing. Twenty-two, husky, drives a dark blue 'fifty-seven Impala."

"What's that got to do with me?"

"I was told he came up here to see you last Friday."

"Then you got told wrong."

"You haven't seen him recently?"

"Nobody comes to see me without they're invited. Nobody."

"That's not what I asked you, Gus."

"Mr. Mayerhof. Nobody calls me Gus unless I say so."

The new headache had put Runyon in a bleak, dark mood. He didn't like pit bulls; he didn't like hard-ass pot growers with shotguns; he didn't like the situation he'd let himself into. And he didn't like having to put the kind of tight hold on himself that Mayerhof had on the dog, even if it was the only option given the circumstances. He said, slow and reasonable, "I don't want much from you, Mr. Mayerhof. Why not just give it to me and I'll be on my way."

"Yeah? Why should I?"

"Be in your best interest."

"Who says so?"

"I say so. My name's Runyon, Jake Runyon."

"Fuck Jake Runyon," Mayerhof said. "You're a trespasser, not a cop."

"Close enough to a cop."

". . . What's that mean?"

"Private investigator. Close ties to the law."

"Bullshit."

"I can show you my license."

"Fuck your license."

The leash on Runyon's temper was starting to fray. "Look, Mayerhof, I didn't come here to make trouble for you. It's none of my business what you do for a living, but I can make it my business if you push me. I can make it the law's business."

"Not if you don't leave here in one piece," Mayerhof said. His body turned slightly as he spoke; the shotgun barrel came up on a level with Runyon's face framed in the open window. His glare was as malevolent as the pit bull's.

"Cold-blooded murder? I don't think so. People know I'm here. How do you suppose I got your name, found out where you live?"

"You never heard of self-defense? Man's got a right to defend his property against trespassers."

"Not when they're sitting inside a car."

"Say you threatened me. Nobody here to call me a liar."

"There'd still be an investigation. How're you going to hide what you grow and sell up here?"

"So maybe you just disappear, you and your car both. Happens all the time in country like this."

"All right then, go ahead and shoot me. But do it quick, Mayerhof. I've got a .357 Magnum in here and the longer you wait, the better my chances of using it. Miss me and I'll blow your head off before you can lever up another shell. The dog's head, too, if you try to let it do the job for you."

"Bullshit."

"I'm a good fast shot, better than you are one-handed with a pump gun, faster than a pit bull can jump through a car window. I was on the Seattle PD for twelve years. Give me the chance and I won't miss."

Standoff. But it was the kind that couldn't last very long. If he'd gauged Mayerhof wrong, he could get himself killed right here and now—put an end to his misery. He cared and he didn't care at the same time. But he hadn't misread the man. He'd had confrontations with dozens of Gus Mayerhofs over the years, the petty criminals with hard-as-nails exteriors and guts that melted and ran when push came to shove.

Nothing changed in Mayerhof's expression and he didn't break eye contact, but inside of thirty seconds the shotgun barrel moved slowly off dead aim until it was pointing at the Ford's sideview mirror. He said, "You got two minutes to ask your questions and haul ass out of here."

"Jerry Belsize. You know him or don't you?"

"I got no memory for names."

"That's not an answer."

"Only answer you're gonna get."

"How often does he come here?"

"Who says he was ever here? Not me."

"When was the last time you saw him?"

Shrug. "Real scarce cars, 'fifty-seven Chevys."

"You better not be jerking me around, Mayerhof."

"And you better not make trouble for me, man. I ain't no backwoods hick. I got friends do me any favor I ask."

"Sure you have."

Mayerhof relaxed his grip on the chain slightly. The dog tensed and began to growl. "Two minutes about up."

Runyon let him have another ten seconds of stare before he put the Ford in gear and backed up. In his rearview mirror as he turned around, he saw Mayerhof and the dog still occupying the same piece of ground, neither of them moving, like sculpted juts of granite among the corpses and skeletons. His shoulder muscles didn't loosen until he was over the rise and through the woods.

Had Mayerhof been lying? Didn't figure that way. Nothing in it for him if he wanted to avoid trouble. Nothing for Brody or the fat woman in the general store or the saloon bunch in lying, either. So Belsize not only hadn't come up to the mountains to hide out; he also hadn't been here last Friday buying pot or having car trouble. Then where was he all that day? Why had he lied to his girlfriend? Why had he left the migrant camp so suddenly and where was he now?

Maybe Rinniak and Sandra Parnell were wrong about the kid. Maybe Jerry Belsize wasn't so innocent after all.

12

FIREBUG

Burn!

Come on come on come on—*burn!*

"What's taking so long? You sure you set the timer right?"

"I know how to do it, don't I?"

"It's been fifteen minutes already."

"I set it for twenty. I just wanted to be sure we had enough time."

"Shit. Fifteen was all we needed. What's the matter with you?"

"You know what the matter is. I just don't think we should be doing this again so soon."

"Why not? You like it as much as I do."

"I've got a bad feeling, that's all. So soon after . . . Manuel."

Burn, damn you, burn!

"We had to kill him. We didn't have any choice."

"I know, but God, I can still see his face. It makes me sick."

"Everything makes you sick. Here, smoke a joint, get calmed down."

"I don't want one right now."

"It's better when you're high, you know that."

"I'll just take a hit off yours. . . ."

"No. Fire up your own."

Small flame, hot, bright, but gone too quick.

"Doesn't it bother you? A little?"

"What?"

"What we did to Manuel."

"No. I'm just glad he came to us first. If he hadn't . . ."

"I keep having nightmares about it. The sound when you hit him with the board, the blood, the way his head looked. And his face after we dragged him up on the rope . . . we didn't have to do *that*."

"I had to. I never saw anybody hanging before. Besides, it wasn't as messy as beating his head in."

"He was already dead, wasn't he?"

"No, he wasn't. He was still breathing."

"Oh Jesus!"

"Why do you think he danced like he did when we pulled him up, why his tongue turned all black? He strangled on that rope."

"Don't!"

"You're a baby, baby."

"I can't help it. It took so long, we almost didn't get

away after you hit that detective. You didn't have to hit him; he didn't know we were there."

"I wanted to hit him. So I did."

"He'd be gone by now if you hadn't. He scares me. He's not stupid. What if he—?"

"Not stupid, but not as smart as I am. None of them are."

"But if we keep on the way we have been—"

"We're not going to."

"We're not? No lie?"

"We're going to get even more creative. More fun, more payback."

"Oh God, fun. Do we *have* to . . . you know?"

"We've already done it. The fire's just the finishing touch."

"I don't think I want to be there. . . ."

"Well, you're going to. You know you always do what I want you to."

"I know, but—"

"Say it."

". . . I always do what you want me to."

"Tell me why."

"You know why."

"I want to hear you say it."

"I love you."

"Again."

"I love you."

"I love you, too. Most of the time. Hey, you know what would've been really cool? If we could've hung Runyon, too. Right next to Manuel, side by side, like in those old cowboy flicks."

"That's gross! Sometimes . . ."

"Sometimes what?"

"*You* scare me. You're so . . ."

"So what? Crazy? Maybe I am; I don't care. Taking risks, having fun, getting even, that's what it's all about."

"Sooner or later we're gonna get caught."

"No, we're not."

"We almost did already. I almost did. If you get any more out of control—"

"I'm not out of control! Don't say that to me!"

"Ow! No, don't hit me again—"

"I will if you give me any more shit like that."

"I won't, baby, I'm sorry."

"Why doesn't that fucking timer go off? Did you pour kerosene inside the trailer like I told you to?"

"Yeah."

"Leave trails to the other cabins?"

"Yes, yes, I told you I did."

"It's going to be a real big fire. Big and hot, bigger and hotter than the school—remember the school? Last longer, too, hours maybe. All the dry grass out here, it'll burn fast."

"What if it spreads this way, climbs up this hill?"

"It won't. There's not much wind and it's blowing away from us."

"Somebody could see us up here—"

Whoosh!

There it goes! About time! *Yes!*

Flames jumping growing racing, eating up the grass, climbing the trailer, climbing the shacks, shooting out windows and roofs. That's it, that's it! Higher, faster, big red tongues licking up the crack of night.

Look at the trailer burn, like a fat bug on a bonfire. Smell the smoke, acid sweet like pot, like devil's perfume. Listen to it crackle, like it's talking to itself, saying burn hotter, faster, burn everything up. Watch it run run run run along the creek and up the cottonwoods and into the orchards, mount the trees one at a time, fuck each one, make it come in a crown of fire.

Somebody's seen it by now, somebody's called 911. Won't be long before the sirens. And then the fire trucks and the firemen and the hoses and the fire laughing at the puny streams of water trying to put it out. And son of a bitch bastard Don Kelso roaring up in his cruiser, I can hardly wait. He won't be swaggering tonight, giving orders, acting like he knows everything and owns the fucking world. You can't give orders to fire. You can't slap fire around and make it behave.

Oh, man, watch it feed, watch it fuck! So hot, so hungry. Swallowing up the camp now, the trees, the fields, the sky, the night, the whole world. Burning everything up. Burning *me* up inside.

"Hey, what're you doing?"

"What do you think I'm doing?"

"No! Not here, not now—"

"Right here, right now."

"We can't, it's crazy, what if somebody sees us—"
"Burn you up, too, burn both of us up together."
"No, baby, please, please—"
"Don't fight me, don't make me hurt you."
Burning up burning up burning up . . .

13

When I came into the offices on Monday morning, Tamara said, "We're not gonna have Jake for a couple of days."

"How come?"

"He called last night, and again a few minutes ago. Man had a rough weekend up north and it's still not done with."

"What happened?"

"Walked blind into a murder and arson case, got himself a bad whack on the head. Guy he was supposed to deliver the subpoena to is missing and the local law thinks it's because he's the perp." She explained the rest of the situation, as Runyon had outlined it to her.

"Christ. How bad's his concussion?"

"Not too serious. He figured he'd be able to leave today, but there was another fire last night—that's how come the second call—and now it looks like he's stuck until tomorrow."

"He need any help from us?"

"He says no."

Cause for concern just the same. Runyon had become an important fit in the short time he'd worked for the agency. He'd put his life and his license on the line for Tamara and me on more than one occasion, and a tight professional bond had developed among the three of us—trust, respect, understanding. That was as far as it went, by tacit consent. He wasn't the kind of man who invited friendship outside the office, or who seemed to need friends at all. Still grieving for his late wife—another reason he had my empathy. I cared about the man, I knew Tamara did, too, and his actions and as much talking as you could get him to do indicated he felt the same way.

"Keep in touch with him. If he needs us, we'll work something out."

"Told him that."

"Okay. Meanwhile, we've got the Ogden investigation to move on."

"Already started," she said. "Last night, after I got back from apartment hunting."

"Didn't tell me you were looking for a new place."

"Yeah, well, about time I had me a Horace-free environment."

"Any luck?"

"Not much so far. One place I liked on Potrero Hill, but it's bigger than I need—three-bedroom flat—and the damn landlord ought to be arrested for extortion, the rent he's asking."

"Seller's market again. We were lucky to get this new office space as cheaply as we did."

"Don't I know it. Maybe I ought to just move my butt in here, save money all around."

She wasn't serious, but I had to look at her closely to make sure. Tamara is the impulsive type, levelheaded most of the time, but every now and then she gets a notion into her head that rattles the hell out of convention.

I told her how I'd spent part of my Sunday, what little I'd found out from T. R. Quentin. She made a note of it to add to the Ogden file; when it comes to business matters, she's pure efficiency.

"Not much on Mathias so far," she said. "Man's personal finances look pretty clean—no debts or overextensions or big investments, nothing that even has much of a built-in risk factor. Real conservative type, at least on the surface. If he's got any vices, they're well hidden."

"Same profile as four years ago. What about RingTech?"

"Solid. Profits up fifteen percent since Mathias took it over four years ago, expansion plans in the works, looks like they're going public pretty soon. Another Donald Trump in the making." One corner of her mouth quirked. "Bet I know who he voted for last election."

"Yeah. So any financial motive appears to be out."

"Looks that way. No need for his wife's assets or the life insurance."

"And he had full control of RingTech even before her death."

"One hundred percent. She wasn't even on the board of directors."

"Doesn't leave us with much," I said. "Except jealousy, if she was involved with another man. Or maniacal possessiveness, if she was planning to leave him."

"Control freaks like him look at their women same as abusive husbands, you know what I'm saying? Possessions. Can't stand to lose the women unless they decide to throw them away themselves. Thousands of assholes like that kill their wives every year. After reading that diary, I can see Mathias as one of 'em."

"Maybe. The two things that argue against it are his apparent conservative nature and his ambition. And Ring-Tech's about to make an IPO, you said. Would a guy with his mind-set, on the cusp of a major step upward in the corporate world, risk everything on a crime of passion?"

"Might if he figured he could get away with it."

"We don't know enough about him; that's the problem. All we have is hunches, biased impressions, a lot of secondhand and four-year-old information."

"Digging as deep as I can."

"I know. I wonder if a face-to-face meeting might help? Form my own impressions."

"How you gonna manage that? Let him know he's being investigated?"

"No," I said, "not exactly. I think maybe there's a better way."

• • •

Nancy Mathias's attorney was Harold Moorehouse, of the firm of Zimmerman, Gorman, and Moorehouse. He was in when I called their offices in Palo Alto, and willing to talk frankly; Celeste Ogden had paved the way with an earlier phone call. But he had little enough to tell me. His client hadn't told him why she wanted to see him or given him any indication of the reason. When she didn't show up for the scheduled appointment, Moorehouse had had his secretary call her home to ask why. The secretary hadn't spoken to her; got an answering machine, left a message. The call wasn't returned.

I said, "Mrs. Mathias sounded upset when she made the appointment, is that right?"

"If I used the word 'upset' to Mrs. Ogden, it was a poor choice."

"What would be a better one?"

"It's difficult to gauge a person's emotional state over the phone. But the word that comes to mind at the moment is 'wounded'."

"How do you mean?"

"As if she'd been badly hurt in some way," Moorehouse said, "and was having difficulty coping with it. I assumed whatever it was, was her reason for wanting to consult with me."

"She didn't give you any idea of what it might be?"

"None. I asked her, of course, but she said she preferred not to discuss the matter over the phone."

"Have you spoken with her husband since her death?"

There was a slight pause before Moorehouse answered. And when he did, his voice had tightened perceptibly. "Twice, as a matter of fact. I called him when I received the news. And we exchanged a few words at the funeral."

"Did you mention her call or the missed appointment?"

"No. It didn't seem appropriate."

"What's your opinion of the man, Mr. Moorehouse?"

"That's not a relevant question," he said.

"Maybe not, but I get the impression you don't much care for him."

"If that's your conclusion." Typical lawyer response.

"May I ask why?"

"Another irrelevant question."

"Not to me."

"I would rather not answer it, just the same."

"I'd really appreciate it if you would. Or at least tell me how you'd characterize him. Off-the-record, of course."

Silence for a few seconds. Then Moorehouse said, "Very well. Cold, indifferent to the feelings of others. The kind of man who has no genuine human emotions, only simulates them."

Perfect thumbnail description of a sociopath.

The San Francisco offices of Pacific Rim Insurance were located in one of the city's downtown landmarks, the Transamerica Pyramid. I walked in there at 12:35, ten minutes early for my appointment with the head of Pacific's Claims Investigation Department, Irv Blaustein.

When you've been in private practice as long as I have

and one of your specialties is freelance work for insurance companies too small or too cheap to maintain an investigative staff of their own, you get to know a lot of people in the industry. Pacific Rim was one of the larger outfits, with their own staff, and while I'd never done a job for them, I'd met Blaustein three or four times during the course of other cases. I knew him well enough to call him and convince him to give up part of his lunch hour on short notice for a consultation. Not that it had taken much convincing; all I'd had to do was mention the possibility of Pacific Rim saving a potful of money.

He didn't keep me waiting. Promptly at 12:45 he appeared in the waiting room and personally conducted me through a rabbit warren of cubicles to his private office. He was about my age, and he moved in a plodding, stooped-over posture as if he had back or spine problems. From this, and his nondescript face and mild manner, you might have taken him for the nonaggressive executive type taking up office space until his retirement. You'd have been wrong. He was a bulldog, one of the most tenacious claims chiefs in the business—a kind of tall, gangly modern version of Barton Keyes, the Edward G. Robinson character in *Double Indemnity*.

Once we were seated with the door closed, he wasted no time getting down to the business at hand. "I looked over the Mathias claim after we spoke on the phone," he said. "It seems reasonably straightforward and aboveboard."

"My client, the deceased's sister, doesn't think so."

"She doesn't believe it was an accidental death?"

"No. She suspects foul play—a murder-for-hire job."

"The husband?"

"Yes. Husband and beneficiary."

"Based on what?"

"A lot of intangibles so far. But enough to convince me that an investigation is worth undertaking."

"I'd like to know what they are."

"I'll have my partner e-mail you a copy of our case file to date."

Blaustein leaned back, elbows on the arms of his chair, fingers steepled. "So what is it you want from us?"

"Question first. Has whoever's handling the claim for you had any personal contact with Brandon Mathias?"

"No. Given the preliminary findings, our man hasn't found it necessary."

"Good. What I'd like to do is interview Mathias myself, get a better handle on the man, probe him a little. I can't just walk in and announce that his sister-in-law hired me to investigate him as a possible homicide suspect; he'd refuse to talk to me. But he isn't likely to refuse to talk to a representative of Pacific Rim."

Blaustein frowned. "We don't hire outside investigators, you know that."

"Sure. And you know my reputation, Irv. I'm not looking to cadge another fee; I don't operate that way. Strictly a quid pro quo favor is what I'm asking."

"I don't know," Blaustein said. "I can't justify misrepresentation."

"It won't be misrepresentation. Call it a sanctioned

smoke screen. I'll make the approach using my own name, give you a full accounting of my conversation with him, and turn over anything my investigation might uncover that has a bearing on his claim."

"Permission to use Pacific's name, that's all you're asking?"

"Onetime usage, right. And for you to back me up if Mathias decides to make a checkup call."

"Why should he? You plan to come on that strong?"

"Not strong enough to get his back up, no," I said. "I'd never do or say anything that would reflect badly on Pacific Rim."

"When are you going to see him?"

"As soon as he's available."

Blaustein thought it over, taking his time. At length he said, as much to himself as to me, "Double indemnity clause. Hundred-thousand-dollar payoff if the claim is valid."

I didn't say anything.

"Well, what the hell, why not," he said. "Just don't make me regret this."

"I won't."

"All right. Consider yourself an unofficial and unpaid Pacific Rim employee for the next forty-eight hours. I'll even give you one of our claims department business cards to cement the deal."

On the way out of the building I rang up Tamara, reported the gist of my conversation with Blaustein, asked her to e-mail him our case file and to call RingTech and make an ASAP appointment with Mathias using Pacific Rim's name. The old secretary-calling-for-her-boss dodge tends to lend weight and urgency, true or false, to business arrangements made by phone.

She called back as I was ransoming the car from the Sutter-Stockton garage. "Four o'clock today," she said. "He's giving you fifteen minutes out of a real tight schedule."

"You talk to him personally?"

"His assistant, Drax. No surprise Nancy Mathias didn't like that dude. He's got a bloodsucker's voice—Bela Lugosi without the heavy accent."

"Uh-huh. I'll see if I can talk to him, too."

"Keep your neck covered if you do."

14

RingTech's headquarters were in an upscale office park off Page Mill Road, just south of the Stanford University campus. Low-slung black granite-and-glass building surrounded on three sides by an acre or so of manicured lawn and shade trees. The fourth side was a parking lot complete with a small section whose slots were labeled **Visitor.**

In the lobby I had to sign in at a security desk, put on a visitor's badge with my name on it, and then pass through a metal detector, all of which made me wonder. Sign-of-the-times precaution? Paranoia on the part of Brandon Mathias? Or did RingTech manufacture something more sensitive than business software?

The place was a beehive; lobby, elevators, second-floor hallways were all crowded with people on the move. There was a sense of urgency in the air, as if everybody was working under some sort of deadline pressure. Gearing up for the imminent IPO, maybe; when a company goes public with its stock, it has to make sure all its contracts are being met on schedule, its research and development and other divisions operating at maximum efficiency.

The executive offices were at the rear. Big anteroom with a receptionist, who checked my badge before she permitted me to pass into an inner waiting room with nobody human in it except me. There was a couch, a matching chair, a table with a coffeepot on a hot plate and a stack of cups ("Please help yourself to coffee; Mr. Mathias will be with you shortly"). No windows and nothing adorning the walls, which gave it the look and feel of a privileged prisoner's cell in a minimum security prison.

I tried sitting down, but the couch was uncomfortable. So I paced around instead, listening to silence—ten paces from wall to wall one way, eight paces the other because of the furniture. It was five past four o'clock, and I'd been there ten minutes and reduced to reading the label on a jar of Maxwell House instant coffee when the door opened and somebody came in and got me.

Not the receptionist and not Brandon Mathias. "I'm Anthony Drax," he said, "Mr. Mathias's assistant. Sorry to keep you waiting, but I'm afraid he's running a bit late this afternoon."

"No problem."

"It shouldn't be too long. He asked me to show you into his office."

Mathias's sanctum was big, windowed on two sides with views of lawn and trees, but as spartanly furnished and functional as the waiting cell. Just the type of no-frills office you'd expect a phlegmatic, dedicated, ambitious business exec to have. Drax indicated a chair to one side of a broad gunmetal gray desk, and when I sat in it he said, "I'll keep you company until Mr. Mathias comes in, if you don't mind."

"Not at all."

He plunked himself down in a matching chair on the other side. I watched him cross one leg over the other and rest both hands comfortably on his knee. He wasn't what I'd expected, given Nancy Mathias's diary entry and Tamara's phone comment earlier. The Dracula comparison was an overheated exaggeration. Tall and lean, all right, with sharp incisors and piercing eyes, but his swarthy skin didn't seem particularly leathery and there was nothing sinister about his appearance or his manner. Rising young executive type, suit and tie, shoes polished to a gloss, fingernails manicured, thinning hair neatly barbered and combed. I didn't much like those eyes—they looked through you, rather than at you, and the irises were a kind of subterranean black—but you can't judge a man on that basis alone.

Pretty soon he said, "Terrible, what happened to Mrs. Mathias. Just terrible."

"Yes, it was."

"I imagine you see a lot of that sort of thing in your business."

"What sort of thing is that?"

"Fatal home accidents."

"We see a lot of alleged accident claims, yes."

"Alleged? I don't understand."

"Not all of them turn out to be accidents."

The black stary eyes narrowed. "You're not suggesting Mrs. Mathias's death wasn't accidental?"

"I'm not suggesting anything," I said.

"The woman was alone behind locked doors when she fell," Drax said. "The police were satisfied."

"The police don't get paid to be skeptical. I do."

"Why are you skeptical?"

"I didn't say I was. I said I get paid to be."

"Then why are you here? What do you want with Mr. Mathias?"

"The answers to a few questions. Clarification of facts."

"What questions? What facts?"

"That's between Mr. Mathias and me."

"He wasn't even in the state when his wife died. You must know that. He was at a business meeting in Chicago."

"So we understand, yes."

"Do you doubt it?"

"I have no reason to doubt it."

"Then why are you here to harass him?"

"Ask questions, Mr. Drax. I don't harass, I investigate."

"He's under a terrible strain as it is," Drax said. "Ring-Tech is expanding, we're about to go public with our stock, and the death of his wife has made a difficult time even twice as bad. Can't you understand that?"

I understood that he'd put the IPO first, Nancy Mathias's death second. I said, "What would you have me do? Rubber-stamp a claim because a man I don't know is going through a difficult time?"

"Brandon Mathias is not just any man. You don't seem to realize that."

"No? Suppose you enlighten me."

"He's a major player in the computer software business and one day he'll be a major player in corporate America." Drax's voice had reverence in it, the kind that is usually accorded to kings and popes. Or to Donald Trump by his underlings.

"A VIP," I said.

"Yes. Exactly. Much too important to be subjected to inconsequentials."

"You consider his wife's death inconsequential?"

"I didn't mean that," Drax said. "I meant your investigation. It's unnecessary and intrusive at such a difficult period in his life."

"That's your opinion."

"It's the opinion of everyone at RingTech."

"But not necessarily mine or Pacific Rim's."

Basilisk stare. Those piercing eyes had a hypnotic quality when emotions ran strong in him. "Are you trying to insinuate that Mr. Mathias had something to do with his wife's death? So you and your company can void his claim?"

"I don't insinuate any more than I harass, Mr. Drax."

"That's what it sounds like to me."

"What you think is irrelevant. Your opinions don't matter."

"You can't talk to me like that. How dare you!"

Nobody had ever said "how dare you!" to me before. I didn't like it much, coming from Drax. I didn't like him much. I told myself it was time to ease off, but I might have pushed him a little further if Brandon Mathias hadn't picked that moment to walk in.

Drax had been leaning forward in his chair, glaring at me; as soon as he saw his employer, he stood up straight as an arrow and drew his shoulders back, the way a soldier does in the presence of big brass. I got up, too, more slowly—more reflex than anything else. As soon as I was on my feet, I wished I'd stayed seated.

The thing was, people would generally snap to attention when Mathias showed up. He was the kind of man who owns a room as soon as he enters it, who expects deference and demands obedience. One good look at him and you knew that. It wasn't a matter of stature—he was an inch or so under six feet, narrow shouldered, small hands and feet, unprepossessing features, with a mop of Ted Kennedy–like brown hair. It was an air of supreme self-confidence, a kind of radiating magnetism. High-level politicians have it. So do what Drax had referred to as major players in corporate America. It can't be faked or manufactured; those who have it are born with it.

Mathias greeted me with a grave smile, an apology—"I'm sorry to be so late; I was detained in a meeting"—and a firm handshake, maintaining eye contact the entire time. The eyes, a deep blue-green, might have had sadness in them, but he didn't look like a grieving widower. Or a businessman under a terrible strain. He looked fit in a dark Armani suit, reasonably well rested, at ease, and in charge. Politicians' charisma, and that was something you could fake. He wore his like a tight-fitting mask. So tight and so seemingly genuine that the iceman underneath was completely hidden.

He dismissed Drax, who left without a word, aiming another glare at me on his way out. Mathias went around behind his desk, sat down when I did. He placed his hands flat on the desktop and leaned forward slightly, letting me have his full attention, waiting for me to open the conversation.

I said, "My condolences on your loss, Mr. Mathias. How are you bearing up?"

"As well as can be expected, thank you."

"I won't keep you long. I just have a few questions."

"Of course."

"Were you and your wife having any problems prior to her death?"

Fastball, high and tight. He didn't even twitch. "Problems?"

"Personal difficulties."

"Why do you ask that?"

"Part of my job. Do you mind answering?"

"No, of course not. Nancy and I were devoted to each other. Our four years together were the happiest of my life."

"So you'd say she was happy, too. Content."

"Very much so."

First lie. And not a small one.

I said, "I understand she was something of a recluse."

"Nancy? Lord, no. She was a very warm, outgoing person."

"But she didn't go out often, stopped seeing all her friends."

"Did her sister tell you that? Celeste Ogden?"

"As a matter of fact, yes."

"Well, you really should take anything that woman says with several grains of salt. Mrs. Ogden disapproved of my marriage to Nancy, disapproved of our lifestyle. She made such an intrusive annoyance of herself that Nancy stopped having anything to do with her." He paused for dramatic effect. "The woman is also a trespasser and a thief."

"Is that right?"

"Oh yes. After Nancy's accident, she illegally entered my home and rummaged through my wife's belongings and removed a number of private papers."

"How do you know this?"

"I discovered the items missing the following day. Found out later she talked the housekeeper into giving her a key. Simple addition."

"Did you confront her?"

"No. She would only have denied it."

"Notify the police?"

"No. It was more an annoyance than anything else and

my time is budgeted to the max as it is. The stolen items weren't important."

"You're sure of that?"

"Absolutely. Household bills and the like. Nancy kept nothing of value in her office."

"I think I'll have a talk with Mrs. Ogden."

"Do that," Mathias said. "But remember those grains of salt. And the fact that she's a thief."

"Let's get back to your wife. What was her mental state in the days prior to her death?"

"I don't understand the question."

"Was she worried about anything? Upset, distracted?"

"Not at all."

"Was she given to mood swings, bouts of depression?"

"Certainly not."

"You left for Chicago the day before she died," I said. "Something might have happened that you're not aware of."

"I spoke to her on the phone the afternoon of her accident. She would have told me if any problem had come up. She was in very good spirits, looking forward to my return."

"Was she expecting a visitor that night?"

"Nancy didn't have nighttime visitors."

"Would she have told you if she was?"

"Certainly. We had no secrets from each other."

Smooth, lying bastard. Looking at him, listening to him, made the palms of my hands itch. "Who else has a key to your house, besides you and the housekeeper?"

"No one else."

"And your wife always kept the doors locked at night when she was alone?"

"Of course she did," Mathias said. "What is the purpose of all these questions? Do you have reason to suspect that Nancy's death was anything other than a tragic accident?"

"No concrete reason."

"But you do suspect it?"

"I suspect the possibility. That's the nature of my job, Mr. Mathias."

"Suicide? That's preposterous, you know. No one in their right mind would attempt suicide by throwing themselves down a flight of stairs—the actuarial probabilties of that happening must be incalculable. My wife was nothing if not sane."

"Suicide isn't the only explanation."

"Foul play? That's just as preposterous, for heaven's sake. The doors and windows were locked; there were no signs of an intruder and nothing missing prior to Celeste Ogden's visit. Nancy would not have opened the door to a stranger or even to someone she knew late at night, and I've already told you that all the keys are accounted for. The Palo Alto police were satisfied. Why aren't you?"

I said nothing. Maybe a silent stare would tweak him a little.

It didn't. He said, "Is it an attempt on the part of your company to deny the insurance claim? If it is . . ."

"Pacific Rim doesn't operate that way. Neither do I."

"Not that I care if the claim is denied," he said. "I already have more money than I will ever be able to spend. I might even withdraw it, to save myself any more anguish, but I won't if you intend to persist in an investigation that has no basis in fact or logic."

"The decision is Pacific Rim's, not mine."

He pretended not to hear that. He was on a roll now. "I've just lost my wife, the only woman I ever loved. Is it too much to ask a little human compassion?"

Anything I said to that would have sounded lame or defensive or both. Mathias knew it as well as I did.

"Yes, I thought as much," he said. He looked pointedly at the slim platinum-gold watch on his wrist. "I have another meeting in five minutes. If you have any more questions, please be brief."

The only thing I had left was thinly guised accusation, and all that would buy me and Pacific Rim was trouble. Mathias figured to be the litigious type; push him too hard and he'd lawyer up fast and furious. Besides, you could interrogate him for days and he'd never admit to anything that wasn't in his own best interest. Like a damn modern politician in that sense, too: never admit wrongdoing, never allow yourself to be held accountable, just stonewall and misdirect and obfuscate.

"Nothing further," I said. "For now."

He stood up in one fluid motion, came around the desk to stand next to my chair. It wasn't to offer to shake hands again; it was to look down on me, literally as well as figuratively. He said, with some of the iceman in his voice, "My secretary will take you out," and left me sitting there as if I were a large piece of trash awaiting removal to the Dumpster.

15

JAKE RUNYON

There wasn't much left of the abandoned migrant workers' camp. Scorched earth, the naked black bones of trees,
burned-out cinder-block and metal husks. The fire trail extended in a wide swath from the side road deep into the
surrounding orchards. Here and there faint wisps of
smoke drifted up and faded, like fog dying in the hot
morning sunlight. A handful of uniformed firefighters
were still on the scene to watch for hot spots, their trucks
and equipment strung out along the roadside. The usual
rubberneckers were there, too, small knots of them standing off at a distance with looks on their faces that were
half-hungry, half-disappointed, because the main show
was over.

Joe Rinniak said, "It could've been a hell of a lot worse.
Not much wind last night. If there had been and the fire

had jumped the county road . . . well, there's a big farm over there, more than a dozen buildings."

"No question it was arson?"

"None. First firefighters to get here said you could smell the kerosene. CDF investigator found two gallon cans in the rubble, just before I called you. Remains of a timer, too, the same kind that was used on the other fires."

"Pretty open out here," Runyon said. "Not many places for a bug to wait and watch his handiwork. Who turned in the alarm?"

"Family across the road. You thinking he doubled back to watch after the fire started? No, the son of a bitch was here the whole time."

"How do you know?"

They were standing on the verge of the side road, near the blackened ruts that had led into the camp. Rinniak turned to point behind them, at a rocky hillock several hundred yards to the southeast. "Up there in those rocks. There's a farm road back behind the hill, can't see it from here—loops around to the county road about a mile south. Easy enough for him to slip away in the confusion, running dark, when he'd had enough."

"Find anything up there?"

"Not much. Nothing that might ID the perp. Flattened grass where the car was parked, among the rocks where he hid to watch. Kelso was the first man up there, early this morning. He may have authority issues, but he's no dummy."

"I don't see him here now."

"Left before I got here. Where to, I don't know. But don't be surprised if he looks you up today."

"I won't be."

"And it won't be for the same reason I called," Rinniak said. "He didn't like you coming out here with Sandra Parnell yesterday. If you'd gone by the book, notified him Saturday night that the girl knew where Jerry Belsize was hiding, Belsize would be in jail now and there wouldn't have been a fire here last night. That's what he thinks."

"Maybe. If Belsize hadn't already disappeared by the time I talked to the Parnell girl. And if he's guilty."

"I'm starting to think Kelso's right about that much. Why would Belsize run if he wasn't guilty?"

"If he's the bug, he didn't run."

"Not before last night, anyway. But if he's still in the area, where? Hell, he had a good hiding place out here."

"Better one picked out somewhere, maybe."

"Could be. This is a big county, a lot of it rural. Planning to torch the camp all along, in that case."

Runyon watched a helmeted CDF investigator poke and prod among the rubble. "Did Kelso arrest Sandra Parnell yesterday?"

"No. He didn't get anything out of her, let her go with a hard warning. Laid down the law to her folks, too, not that it'll do any good. The Parnells aren't your all-American watchdog parents. Father's been out of a job since the olive processors in Stander shut down a year and a half ago, spends most of his time in bars; mother works long hours at two jobs."

Runyon made no comment.

"You spent some time with the girl," Rinniak said. "Think she knows more than she's admitting?"

"Hard to tell. She's hung up on Belsize, and it's pretty obvious she hates and fears Kelso."

"A lot of these kids do. Price he pays for being the way he is."

Price the community at large pays, too, Runyon thought. But he didn't say it.

"I hate cases like this," Rinniak said. "Too much going on under the surface, too much weird. You can't predict what'll happen next. And something sure as hell will, if Belsize or whoever the bug is stays on the loose."

"Agreed."

"Well, maybe we'll get lucky. That's what it's going to take—luck."

Runyon said, "How much longer you going to want me around?"

"As far as I'm concerned, you can head home right now. But it depends on Kelso. Officially I'm his superior officer, but this is his jurisdiction and his record is one of the best in the department. I've got to cut him a certain amount of slack."

"I talked to one of my bosses this morning. They need me back in San Francisco ASAP."

"All right. Stick around today, try not to ruffle Kelso's

feathers, and if there are no more surprises I'll see to it you can leave tomorrow."

Kelso wasn't at the substation in Gray's Landing. The gray-haired officer manning the place didn't know where he was, and the call he put in over the radio at Runyon's request went unanswered. Runyon asked for the deputy's home address; the officer said he couldn't give out that information.

Down the street was an open cafe; Runyon scouted up their public phone and a county directory. D. Kelso, 377 Alderwood Court, GL. So much for pro forma security. There was also a local listing for M.&R. Parnell, the only Parnells in the book: 600 Basalt Street. A Gray's Landing street map at the front of the directory showed him how to get to both addresses. Alderwood Court was closest, just a handful of blocks from downtown. He drove there first.

Cul-de-sac of middle-class houses, the kind popular in rural towns half a century ago—two stories, wraparound or half-wraparound porches, gingerbread trim. Number 377 was painted white with dark blue trim. There was no sign of Kelso's cruiser, but a young woman was just coming through the front gate onto the sidewalk. The daughter, Ashley. Runyon circled around, pulled up next to her, hit the button to lower the passenger side window.

She stopped when he spoke her name, bent to peer inside the car. She was wearing faded Levi's and a khaki shirt with the words "Battle Hardware" stitched over the pocket. The sun caught her midnight black hair and threw off dazzling highlights.

"Well," she said, "look who's here. Hello there."

"I'm looking for your father. Know where I can find him?"

"No. He's supposed to be here right now, giving me a ride to work. I'm gonna be late."

"I'll give you a ride."

She struck a coy pose, one hand on a cocked hip. "Well, gee, I don't know. Daddy says I'm not supposed to get into cars with strange men."

Runyon was in no mood for games. He said, "If you want a ride, get in. Otherwise I'll just keep on looking."

"For other girls to pick up?"

He started to raise the window.

"Okay, okay," Ashley said, "I was just kidding." She got into the car, sat with one knee drawn up and her body turned against the door so she was facing him. "I wish I had a car. Even one like this."

"How come you don't?"

"Daddy won't buy me one; he says I'm too irresponsible. I got a ticket once driving Zach's car, that's why. You remember Zach?"

Runyon nodded.

"I don't make enough money to buy one myself," she said. "Someday, but not yet. Is this the only one you own?"

"Why?"

"It's pretty old. I guess detectives don't make much money."

"Enough. You work at Battle Hardware?"

"Ever since I got out of high school, part-time. Daddy wanted me to go to college, but I didn't have the grades. He says I didn't study hard enough—I guess he's right. I never did like school much."

"Sometimes," Runyon said, "fathers want things from their kids they can't have."

"Sounds like you know from experience. You have kids?"

"One son."

"Is he smart?"

"Yes."

"But he won't give you something you want, right?"

He didn't answer that. "How do I get to the hardware store?"

"It's on Fourth and A, two blocks off Main."

He put the Ford into gear, swung around out of the cul-de-sac.

"It's a shitty job," she said, "but if I couldn't go to college, I had to work and pay my way. Daddy's big on that kind of stuff. Being responsible, a good citizen, a good Christian."

"Sounds like a decent philosophy to me."

"Oh, sure. But strict fathers can be a pain in the ass sometimes. Were you a strict father?"

I never had the chance. But he didn't say it.

Ashley was silent for half a block. Then, "There was another fire last night. You know about it, I guess."

"I was out there a little while ago."

"I heard it burned up the migrant workers' camp and everything around it for half a mile."

"Not quite half a mile. But close enough."

"Jerry must be really crazy, setting another fire so soon."

"If Jerry's guilty."

"Sure he is. Guilty as sin."

"Some people don't think so. Sandra Parnell, for one."

"That's because she's fucking him."

The words were intended to shock; Ashley said them with a sidelong glance. Runyon kept his eyes front.

Ashley sighed. "Poor Sandy, she's not real smart. Where guys are concerned, anyway. She knows some of the things I know about Jerry, but she's still hung up on him."

"What things?"

"You know I dated him for a while, before she did?"

"I heard as much."

"Daddy didn't like him, didn't want me seeing him. Then he caught us fooling around in our house one day and kicked Jerry's ass right out into the street. It was the best thing that could've happened. I knew about Jerry's ugly side; I just didn't know how bad it was."

"Ugly side?"

The flippancy was gone now; her face was serious. "Reckless driving, racing other cars. One night when I was with him he hit a dog on purpose, no lie, just ran it down in the road. He likes to hurt people, too, when he's high on weed."

"Are you saying he hurt you?"

"Hit me a few times when I said or did something to piss him off. Slaps, mostly, but one time with his fist. I had a bruise on my hip that lasted for a week."

"You tell your father about this?"

"Not until after what happened last Friday. I was scared to before, because of what he might do to Jerry."

No wonder Kelso was so hot after the kid. You couldn't blame him . . . if what Ashley said was the truth.

"You said Sandra knows what you know about Jerry. He beat up on her, too?"

"Couple of times, yeah."

"She admit it to your father?"

"He dragged it out of her yesterday."

"What else did she tell him?"

"Nothing. She swears she doesn't know where Jerry's hiding now, but I'm not so sure. Neither is Daddy."

"Where do you think he might be?"

Ashley raised a hand and a pointing finger. "Turn left there at the corner. That's Fourth Street."

Runyon turned left.

"I don't have a clue," she said. "About where Jerry is, I mean. But Daddy thinks he's still around somewhere in the area, that he'll set more fires, hurt more people, if he's not caught pretty soon."

When Runyon stopped in front of Battle Hardware, Ashley gave him a quick smile and a brief thank-you for the ride and hurried into the store without a backward glance. He watched her out of sight before he drove away. Smart-ass seductive on the one hand, grimly serious on the other. And no dummy, poor grades or not.

Question was, was she also a liar?

He had to stop two people to get directions to Basalt Street. Not worth the trouble, as it turned out. When he reached the semi-industrial area on the west side of Highway 5, found the street and the run-down frame house at number 600, there was nobody there to talk to except for a barking German shepherd in a fenced side yard. Father drinking up his unemployment benefits, mother at one of her two jobs, Sandra at the Hair Today Salon where she worked as a stylist. Trying to talk to the Parnell girl in that kind of business environment would be an exercise in futility. He could look her up later in more private surroundings.

Kelso wasn't at the Belsize farm, but he'd been there not long before Runyon's arrival. Mrs. Belsize told him that. She came hurrying from the chicken coop when he rolled into the yard, a big woman in khaki pants and sweat-stained shirt, gray haired, round cheeked, and still angry.

"That deputy," she said, "he poked around all over the place, every building. Thinks we're hiding Jerry somewhere. He's got it in for my boy, for no reason that makes good sense. I don't blame Jerry for running away from him."

"Kelso have a search warrant?"

"No. Did he need one?"

"To conduct a search of your property he did."

"Well, I wish we'd known that. John would've run him off damn quick."

"Where's your husband now, Mrs. Belsize?"

"Back in the corral with the horses. You want him?"

"Not necessarily."

"What're you doing here anyhow?" she demanded. "You think we've got Jerry hid up in the hayloft, too?"

"I thought Kelso might be here."

"Why you looking for him?"

"Because he's looking for me."

His bandage seemed to register on her for the first time. Her face softened slightly; so did her voice. "How's your head? That blow give you a concussion, they told us."

"Mild one. I'm all right now."

"Well, I'm glad to hear it. You don't blame us for what happened?"

"Not at all."

"Last thing we need is some damn personal injury lawsuit."

"Don't worry, I'm not litigious."

"Glad to hear that, too." Heavy sigh. "Shame you didn't get here with that subpoena of yours half an hour sooner on Friday night. Maybe poor Manny'd still be alive."

Runyon said he wished he had, too.

"A subpoena, of all things. As if Jerry don't have enough grief."

"It's just a piece of paper requiring him to appear in court, that's all."

"I know that. Don't you think I know that?" She sighed again, wiped her damp face with a man's handkerchief. Her gaze seemed drawn to the larger of the two barns. "Why anybody would do such a terrible thing, go to all that trouble to get John and me away from here so they could kill Manny—that's what I don't understand. He was a good man, a family man. Got along with everybody."

"Including your son."

"They were friends, by God. Jerry no more done that to Manny than he can fly like a bird."

"She's right, mister," John Belsize said. "Make no mistake about it."

Runyon had seen him coming, the man's slatlike body moving in long, hard strides across the yard. He stopped next to his wife. They were about the same height, but she was at least a foot wider. His stance was both aggressive and protective, which seemed to make him the dominant partner.

"I don't doubt you believe your son is innocent, Mr. Belsize."

"Meaning you do doubt he is."

"I don't have an opinion one way or the other. What I think doesn't matter anyway."

"That's for goddamn sure."

She said, "John," not loud or sharp but with iron in her tone. It scraped the edge off Belsize's temper; you could see him back off. Runyon revised his opinion as to which of them was dominant.

"We don't know where Jerry is," Belsize said, evenly this time. "That's what we told Kelso and that's the truth."

"What would you do if you did?"

"Don't make any difference because we don't."

"You was out at the workers' camp yesterday, before the fire," the woman said. "Deputy told us you was."

"I was there."

"With that girl, Sandra Parnell."

"Yes."

"Told us there was marijuana in that trailer where Jerry was hiding," Belsize said. "Claimed Jerry was smoking dope out there. I don't believe it. His mother don't, neither."

"There were roach butts in the trailer. I saw them myself."

"Somebody else smoked them. Jerry's a good boy, clean-cut. Don't you suppose we'd know it if he was the kind of wild, crazy kid Kelso says he is?"

"What I don't understand," Mrs. Belsize said, "is why he went to that girl for help."

Runyon said, "She's his girlfriend."

"No, she ain't. Not anymore."

"Since when?"

"Couple, three weeks ago. He broke up with her."

"Good thing, too," Belsize said. "I never liked her much."

"No? Why not?"

"Just didn't. Fast. One look at her, you knew she'd spread her legs for anybody that asked."

"John."

He shut up again.

Runyon asked, "Why did Jerry break up with her?"

"He wouldn't say," Mrs. Belsize said. "Just said he found out some things and she wasn't the girl he thought she was and he didn't want nothing more to do with her."

"He was real angry about it, too," Belsize said. "So if he was scared enough to hide from Kelso, how come he went to the Parnell girl instead of us? Why'd he put his trust back in her all of a sudden?"

16

Philomena Ruiz lived in East Palo Alto, on a shabby street a block and a half from Highway 101. Mixed neighborhood, Hispanic and black. Small, old, close-packed houses with tiny yards, many of them barren except for scatters of kids' toys. When I got out of the car I could hear the constant thrum of freeway traffic, smell the faint stink of exhaust emissions and diesel fumes.

A youth about sixteen sporting a sparse patch of chin whiskers opened the door to the Ruiz house. The suspicious look he gave me didn't go away when I asked for Mrs. Ruiz.

"Ma ain't here," he said. "She's working."

"When will she be home?"

"Six thirty, seven."

"I'll stop by again around seven thirty."

"Nah. Seven thirty's when we eat."

"I'll make it around seven then." I handed him one of

my business cards. He looked at it as if he'd been presented with a small dead animal of unknown origin. "Tell her it's about Mrs. Mathias."

"Who?"

"Mrs. Nancy Mathias. One of her employers."

"Yeah," he said, and shut the door in my face.

I drove back across the freeway into Palo Alto. It was like crossing a thin line of demarcation between poverty and affluence. Over here there were stately homes on large lots. Wide lawns, gardens, plenty of shade trees; fences, and locked gates. No wonder East Palo Alto was a simmering pot of anger and resentment and despair that now and then spilled over into violence. You couldn't blame the mostly poor residents, living as close as they did to all the things they could never have, the lives they could never lead. All those hungry faces pressed against an invisible glass wall peppered with invisible signs: Look, but don't touch. Keep out except by daylight invitation.

The Mathias home was on a long block strung with venerable old elms that gave it a parklike atmosphere. Mediterranean style, two stories, decorative wrought-iron balconies, fronted by a barbered lawn surrounded by six-foot privet hedges. The circular driveway was empty; so was the extension of it alongside that led back to a two-car garage. No sign of life on the property; too soon for Mathias to be home. If he spent much time here at all these days. For all I knew he slept in his office at RingTech, to make it easier to manage his pressing and oh-so-stressful business affairs.

I parked under one of the curbside elms and set out to canvass the neighbors. There were five houses on the south side of the block, four on the north side with the Mathias pile in the middle; I started with the ones flanking it and then moved across the street. No answers at two places, one of them occupied—lights glowing faintly behind drawn curtains, a car sitting in the drive. Only a little after five thirty, broad daylight, and the people still hid themselves behind closed and no doubt locked doors. Fear of strangers, even a sixty-two-year-old man wearing a conservative suit and tie, fear of home invasion, fear of solicitors after their money, just plain fear. Not a good way to live, even in these parlous times.

One of those who did answer their doors wouldn't talk to me, looked at me with the same sort of suspicion as the Ruiz kid and then brushed me off with an "I'm busy right now" excuse. Another demanded to know why he was being bothered with "old business." A third gave me a couple of minutes to ask my questions but had nothing to tell me about Nancy Mathias or the night she died. Hardly knew her, kept to herself, used to be friendly until she remarried; didn't see anything, didn't hear anything, don't know anything.

Then, on the sixth try, I got lucky.

It was the next to last house on the south side, a larger than average bungalow surrounded by neatly tended formal gardens. It had a deep front porch covered by the kind of motor-driven Plexiglas awning that can be lowered in bad weather and furnished with a couple of old, comfortable armchairs. A frail-looking woman in her late seventies sat in one of the armchairs, a robe over her lap and a tortoiseshell cat curled up on it. She was more than willing to talk. She introduced herself—Mrs. Mary Conti— invited me to sit down, asked if I'd like something to drink, commented on the nice late-summer weather. At first I thought she was the garrulous type, but that wasn't it at all.

"I'm a widow," she said. "I lost my husband, Adam, last October. Heart trouble; he was bedridden for nearly a year before he finally passed on. We were married fifty-two years, he was a wonderful man. We used to sit out here together on summer evenings before he became ill. My daughter keeps after me to sell the house and move in with her, but I can't bring myself to do that. I've lived here for forty years, both my children were born here. How can I sell all those wonderful memories?"

Lonely. Sad and lonely.

Gently I steered the conversation around to the Mathiases. Oh yes, she said, she knew poor Nancy. Not well, hadn't seen much of her in recent years, but she was a good neighbor, always had a kind word. Her new husband? Mrs. Conti had waved to him once or twice, but he hadn't waved back. He seemed a very dour sort of man, she said, but then she really didn't know him.

Nothing in any of that. But when I asked her about the night Nancy Mathias had died, I got some of what I was looking for.

"Oh yes, I remember that night," she said. "It was very warm, a beautiful night, so many stars. Just the kind of night Adam would have loved. Big Girl and I sat out here until quite late—this is Big Girl, my tortie; she's a terrible slug, isn't she?"

"A beauty, though. How late did you sit out that night, Mrs. Conti?"

"Oh, it must have been almost eleven before I went in. Yes, almost eleven."

"Did you happen to see or hear anything unusual?"

"Unusual?"

"At or near the Mathias house. Someone entering the property."

"Well, you know, I did see someone, but I'm not sure if he went to the Mathiases' or one of the other houses. The elms throw out heavy shadows, and my vision isn't what it used to be."

"Man or woman?"

"A man. Yes, I'm sure it was."

"What time was that?"

"Oh, it must have been about ten o'clock. It seemed odd to me because it was late for visitors and because of where he parked his car. The people who live on our block all park in their driveways or garages, not at the curb."

"Where did this man park?"

"Right across the street."

"And he walked from there to the Mathias house?"

"In that direction, yes, he did."

I looked across toward the Mathias house. The privet hedges blocked any view of the front entrance. "Could he have turned in at their gate?"

"He may have. I'm just not sure."

"Did any lights come on in the Mathias house?"

". . . No. None that weren't already on."

"Which lights were already on?"

"The night-light over the door. It's always on after dark. Some sort of timer, I believe. And a light in the room above. Mrs. Mathias's study."

"How do you know that's her study?"

"Oh, I've seen her working in there many times. Adam and I used to take evening walks around the neighborhood. Sometimes she would wave to us. That was when she was married to Mr. Ring."

"Did you see the man again, the one who parked across the street?"

"Not for some time."

"How much time?"

"It must have been half an hour or more."

"Could you tell where he came from?"

"No. He was just there when I glanced up, in the shadows. He seemed to be in a hurry, now that I think of it. Very long strides. Adam used to walk that way—long, swinging strides. I had to practically run to keep up with him."

"What kind of car did he have?"

"Adam?"

"No, ma'am. The man, the stranger."

"I don't know very much about cars, I'm afraid."

"Small, large? Two-door, four-door?"

"Well, it was small. Sort of . . . what's the phrase? Low-slung?"

"Yes. A sports car?"

"That's right. A sports car."

"Dark or light colored?"

"Light colored. There was a bit of moon and its hood and top gleamed and I remember it made me think of quicksilver."

"So it could have been silver."

"Yes. Yes, it could."

"About the man himself. Did you get a clear look at him?"

"Not very clear, I'm afraid. His coat collar was pulled up."

"Did you have an impression of height, weight? Big, small, thin, fat?"

Mrs. Conti worked her memory, one hand stroking the old cat on her lap until Big Girl made a burbling sound like water boiling. "Well, he wasn't fat. Tall? No, not really. But not short, either. . . . I'm sorry, the only image I have in my mind is of a moving shape."

"Could you estimate his age?"

"No . . . except that he seemed young to me. He moved the way a young man does, if you know what I mean."

"Yes, ma'am. Did you tell the police about him?"

"The police? Why, no. No one from the police came to see me."

No surprise there. A woman dies from a fall inside a locked house, with no signs of forced entry. Verdict from the beginning: accident. None of the investigators had seen a need to canvass the neighbors, so they hadn't bothered.

Mrs. Conti said, "Should I call and tell them?"

"No, that isn't necessary."

"But if you believe that man had something to do with poor Mrs. Mathias's accident . . . That is why you're investigating, isn't it?"

"It's part of my investigation, yes. If I find out that the man you saw was responsible, I'll contact the police myself." Before I got to my feet I reached over and rubbed the tortoiseshell's ears. "Thanks so much, Mrs. Conti. You've been a huge help."

"Have I? I'm so glad. I don't have much opportunity to be helpful to anyone since Adam passed on. My children don't need me anymore. It's I who need them. Isn't that sad?"

Very sad.

And very lonely.

Gaunt. Overworked. Nervous. Those were the three descriptive adjectives that came to mind on my first look at Philomena Ruiz. She was not much more than forty, but her black hair was already streaked with gray and the lines in her face were etched deep. She hadn't been home long when I got there a couple of minutes past seven; she still wore work shoes and a twinged expression when she moved, as though her legs bothered her and she hadn't had a chance to sit down yet.

In the doorway, after I explained that I was working for Celeste Ogden, she said, "I told everything I know to the police. And to Mrs. Ogden when she came to see me."

"I'm sure you did. I just have a few questions—I won't take up much of your time."

She let me come in, with a certain amount of resignation, and conducted me into a tidy living room packed with old, well-used furniture. The chin-whiskered teenager hovered around us, but not in a protective way. When Mrs. Ruiz and I were seated, the kid said rudely, "*No te pases tanto tiempo con ese anglo viejo y gordo. Tengo hambre y quiero mi comida.*"

My Spanish is rusty, but not that rusty. What I said to him came out pretty quick, if not particularly fluid: "*Ciudado con lo que dices, jovencito. Deberias mostrar mas respector a tus mayors.*"

He blinked at me, openmouthed. Mrs. Ruiz seemed to be trying to hide a smile behind a raised hand. In sharper terms she told him the same as I had, to show some respect for his elders, and also to go fetch his own dinner for a change. He beat it out of there in a hurry. When he was gone she used more formal language to apologize for his rudeness and to say, politely, that I spoke Spanish very well. I thanked her; but my command wasn't all that good, I said, and would she mind if we had our conversation in English.

"What is it you wish to know?"

"Well, to begin with, how long did you work for Mrs. Mathias?"

"Nine years. One full day, one half day, every week."

"Was she usually home when you were there?"

"Not when she was married to Mr. Ring. She was very busy at that time—she had many friends, many activities."

"And after she married Mr. Mathias?"

"Then she was home often when I came."

"What did the two of you talk about?"

"My work."

"Personal matters? Did she confide in you?"

"No. Never. We spoke only of my work and things of no importance."

"She never said anything about her relationship with Mr. Mathias?"

"No. Never."

"What's your opinion of the man?"

"I do not know him. I met him only a few times."

"How did he treat you?"

No response.

"Mrs. Ruiz?"

"As some men treat their servants," she said. She said it without inflection, but there was an undercurrent of bitterness in the words. "As if only he was a child of God."

"Did he treat Mrs. Mathias as a man should treat his wife—as a friend, an equal?"

"No. I do not think so."

"Yet she never complained about him."

"She was a woman in love. Women in love do not complain to those who work for them."

"Do you think she was still in love with him at the time of her death?"

Long pause before Mrs. Ruiz said, "Perhaps not."

"Do you have any idea what happened to change her feelings toward her husband?"

"No."

"The last few times you saw her," I said. "Did she seem different to you, as if something was weighing heavily on her mind?"

"Yes. I thought so."

"Do you have any idea what it was?"

"No. But her headaches seemed worse . . . you know she have bad headaches?"

"Migraines, yes."

"She suffered very much from them."

"Was she seeing a doctor about the headaches?"

"I asked her the last time. A doctor in San Francisco, she said."

"San Francisco?"

"A specialist."

"What kind of specialist?"

"She didn't say."

"Did she mention his name?"

"No."

"Or how long she'd been seeing him?"

"No."

That was all Mrs. Ruiz had to tell me. I left her to her rude son and her dinner, headed for home and a late dinner of my own.

Making progress. But even so, I didn't have a good feeling about the direction we were heading. A case like this one is like driving through a bad neighborhood at night: the streets seem familiar and you're pretty sure you're on the right one, but your instincts keep telling you that sooner or later you'll come to a dead end.

17

Conflicting reports, conflicting images. Every time somebody handed him a verbal picture of Jerry Belsize, it was as if he was looking at the same person with a different face. Like the picture of Dorian Gray. And now the same thing was happening with Sandra Parnell.

The girl was Belsize's devoted soul mate, the one person he was able to turn to in a time of crisis. She wasn't the girl he thought she was and he didn't want anything more to do with her. She was decent, loyal. She was a dope-smoking slut. She was strong willed, with Jerry's best interests at heart. She was a weak and easily fooled punching bag.

It was even worse with Belsize. He was an innocent victim of circumstance. He was guilty as hell. He was a good, clean-cut kid who got along with everybody. He was a wild and crazy kid who bought and distributed marijuana, drove like a maniac, ran down dogs for the thrill of it. He got along fine with Manuel Silvera. He murdered Silvera in cold blood in a particularly vicious way. He treated his girlfriends in a normal fashion. He was a borderline rapist who slapped them around when he got high. He was good; he was evil; he was a little bit of everything in between.

More: He spent all day Friday in Lost Bar, buying half a kilo of weed from Gus Mayerhof and getting his car fixed. He wasn't in Lost Bar at all on Friday. He was a regular customer of Mayerhof's. Mayerhof didn't know him from Adam's off ox. He was so afraid of Kelso he'd opted to hide out at the migrant camp rather than go home and proclaim his innocence. He left the camp for no apparent reason and went somewhere else. He torched the camp. He didn't torch the camp.

What was fact and what was fiction?

Which was the real Sandra Parnell, which the real Jerry Belsize?

There were no other cars in the Gasco station when Runyon drove in. He parked alongside the convenience store, went inside. The red-haired kid with the dim eyes, Bob Varley, was behind the counter looking hot and bored. The place had neither air-conditioning nor ceiling fans and the temperature outside had climbed up into the nineties again.

Runyon said, "Talk to you for a minute?" and introduced himself. But he needn't have bothered.

Varley said, "Yeah, I know who you are."

"No secrets in a small town."

"Yeah."

"I understand you and Jerry Belsize are pretty good friends."

The kid quit making eye contact. Not that it mattered. You couldn't read anything by watching his eyes. They were like a cat's, more mirrors than windows, and even if you could see through them, all you'd be looking at was mostly empty rooms.

"We hung out together sometimes," he said. "But I don't know where he is and I don't know nothing about those fires. I already told Deputy Kelso that."

"You think Jerry's guilty, Bob?"

"I dunno. Everybody says he is."

"Not everybody. His parents don't believe he's capable of setting fires, hurting people."

"Yeah, well, they're his parents, you know?"

"What kind of guy do you think he is?"

"Jerry? A good guy. We get along real good. He don't treat me like some people do. I mean, I know I'm not smart, but that don't matter to him."

"What do the two of you do when you hang out?"

"Do?"

"Chase girls, drink some beer, drag race?"

"Nah, we don't race."

"I heard Jerry likes to drive fast, run down animals that get in his way."

"What? Hey. That's bullshit, man."

"Smoke some dope now and then?"

"I never smoked no dope."

That was a lie. Varley would never be a good liar; it made him turn shifty and furtive.

Runyon said, "Jerry does, though. Supplies weed to his friends, gets it from a German farmer up in Lost Bar."

"He don't. That's more bullshit."

"Come on, Bob. It's no big deal. Everybody smokes pot now and then."

"Yeah, well."

"Jerry's ex-girlfriend does and she's not afraid to admit it."

"What ex-girlfriend?"

"Sandra Parnell."

"She's not an ex."

"His mother says they broke up two or three weeks ago. Not so?"

"Jerry never said nothing about it to me."

"And he would if it were true?"

"I guess he would. Sure, why not?"

"Why would they bust up, if they did?"

"I dunno. They been together a long time."

"Jerry smack her around much?"

"Huh?"

"You know, hit her when he was mad. He likes to play rough, doesn't he?"

"Nah. Who told you that?"

"Maybe he found another girl he liked better. Maybe that's why he broke up with Sandra."

"He didn't care about no other girl."

"Maybe she found somebody else. Pretty hot stuff, I hear."

"Who? Sandra?"

"Made it with a lot of guys."

"She's not like that. Jerry wouldn't stand for that."

"How about before she started going with him?"

"Nah. She never screwed around, not like some girls."

"What's she like then?"

"Oh, you know. Cool."

"Ashley Kelso cool, too?"

Varley began to tighten up; you could see it happening, a kind of ripple effect from his body down his arms and on up to his mouth and chin. "How come you're asking about her?"

"Don't worry, Bob. Anything you tell me won't get back to her father. Strictly between us."

"Yeah, sure."

"No lie. I'm not looking to get anybody into trouble."

"Then why you ask so many questions?"

"I'm a detective. Detectives ask questions. Like on TV, you know?"

"Yeah."

"So tell me about Ashley. What's she like?"

"She's okay. She's friends with Sandra."

"Is that right?"

"Yeah. They hang out sometimes, like me and Jerry."

"She used to go with Jerry, right?"

Varley shifted his weight from one foot to the other.

An SUV came rumbling into the station; he looked out through the window, watching as it pulled up to one of the forward pumps.

"Bob?"

"What?"

"Ashley and Jerry."

"What about 'em?"

"They went together for a while, until her father caught them fooling around and kicked Jerry's ass."

"I guess so. Yeah."

"How'd Jerry feel about that?"

"Nobody likes to get his ass kicked."

"I meant about not being able to go with Ashley anymore."

"He didn't care too much. They was gonna break up anyway."

"How come? Because of Sandra?"

"I dunno."

"So he didn't keep seeing Ashley on the sly?"

"Nah. She wanted to, but he didn't."

"She must've been pretty hung up on him."

"I guess so. For a while."

"When did she start going with Zach Battle?"

"She don't go with Zach. He wants her to, but she just wants to drive his car. She don't have her own car."

"How soon did Jerry and Sandra start going together? Right after he and Ashley broke up?"

"Not right after. Pretty soon."

"How did Ashley feel about that?"

"I dunno."

"Put a strain on her friendship with Sandra?"

"Why ask me, man? I don't know Ashley real well."

"Never dated her yourself?"

"You kidding? She don't want nothing to do with a guy like me."

"Sandra doesn't feel that way, does she?"

"Yeah, she does. None of the girls like me much; they all think I'm just a big dummy." The hurt showed in the abrupt clenching of his hands, the quick twist of his mouth.

End of interview. It would've been even if the driver of the SUV hadn't come in just then to pay for his fill-up. The sad cases like Bob Varley were responsive enough until you touched a nerve; then they closed off entirely, retreated into the dimly lit rooms behind their eyes.

He didn't find Kelso. It was Kelso, after a while, who found him.

He was feeling a little woozy when he left the service station. The thick heat and the fact that he hadn't eaten all day; Rinniak's call had dragged him out of the motel before he'd had a chance for breakfast. There was a Chinese restaurant downtown he'd noticed when he dropped off Ashley Kelso; he drove there first, ate most of a tasteless plate of fried rice with shrimp. Bad choice. The food lay heavy in his stomach before he was out the door, gave him gas and queasiness. His head had begun to ache again, too.

He'd intended to stop by the sheriff's substation again. Instead he went to the motel. Two more messages waiting.

The first was from the same reporter who'd called yesterday, sounding pissed at having been ignored. He'd be even more pissed tomorrow. The second, clocked in at 10:20, was from Mayor Carl Battle. Would Mr. Runyon please stop and see him, at either Battle Hardware or the mayor's office at city hall, before he left Gray's Landing? Not today, Mr. Runyon wouldn't. Tomorrow morning was soon enough.

He found a packet of Alka-Seltzer in his kit, swallowed a Vicodin tablet with the fizz. Stripped to his shorts and lay down in the darkened room with the air conditioner cranked up high. The idea was to rest until his gut and his head were right again, but it wasn't long before he dozed off.

A persistent hammering on the door woke him. The bedside clock said it was after five—he'd been out nearly three hours. Groggy, sweaty, but the physical symptoms seemed to have abated. The banging on the door continued. He thought about putting on his pants and shirt, said the hell with it. He went over in his underwear and looked through the peephole in the door before he opened up.

"It's about time," Kelso said.

"I was asleep."

"I want to talk to you."

"So talk."

"Not like this. Inside."

Runyon backed up as the deputy crowded in and shut the door, not quietly. He sat on the bed, rubbed his face in his hands to clear away the last of the cobwebs. Kelso stood as he had in the Redding hospital, flat-footed, jut jawed, one hand resting on the butt of his service revolver.

He said, "What's the idea, questioning my daughter?"

"You make it sound like an interrogation."

"I asked you a question."

"I went by your place looking for you. She—"

"How'd you know where I live?"

"You're listed in the phone book," Runyon said. The air-conditioning had chilled the sweat on him; he reached for his shirt. "Ashley was on her way to work. I offered her a ride; we talked some on the way. That's all."

"Personal things. About her and Belsize. Matters that are none of your business."

"That's a matter of opinion."

"I don't like it when a cheap private detective comes around my town—"

"*Your* town?"

"—and bothers my daughter and a lot of other people with questions about a felony investigation."

"One that I happen to be involved in."

"Not directly and not officially. Didn't I tell you before to keep out of it? Who do you think you are?"

"A concerned citizen. A cheap detective with a subpoena that I still haven't served."

"The devil with your subpoena. I don't care about that; it's not important anymore. What I care about is a psycho murderer on the loose. And the last thing I need is an outsider getting in the way."

"Rinniak doesn't think I'm in the way," Runyon said.

"I don't care what Rinniak thinks. He doesn't live in this town, he doesn't know Belsize the way I do."

Runyon was still a little logy; his reponse was less politic than it should have have been. "Or have a personal grudge against a kid who's yet to be proven guilty."

Kelso's mouth thinned to a white slash. "Unprofessional bias? Is that what you're accusing me of?"

"I'm not accusing you of anything. Just stating an obvious fact."

"Based on what? What you dragged out of my daughter?"

"You haven't made a secret of your feelings about Belsize."

"I don't let my personal feelings get in the way of doing my job," Kelso said angrily. "I go by evidence, and the evidence in this case points to Belsize."

"Circumstantially, maybe."

"No maybes about it."

"No evidence at all that he set the fire last night."

"Except it was where he was hiding out."

"Why would he go back there and torch the camp?"

"Because he's barn-owl crazy, that's why."

"One man's opinion."

"All right, that's enough. I've had all the interference I'm going to take from you. I want you out of Gray's Landing. And I don't want you talking to anybody else about Belsize or the fires on the way. Do I make myself clear?"

"Clear."

"If you're not gone by tomorrow, I'll slap you with an

obstruction charge. I'm not just blowing smoke—I mean what I say."

When he was alone again Runyon finished buttoning his shirt, put on his trousers. There was anger in him, too, a slow simmer of it. The smart thing to do was pack up and head back to San Francisco right now; he was rested enough for the long drive. He could be at his apartment by ten o'clock, be available for work early tomorrow morning. But he didn't feel like doing the smart thing. He was tired of being banged up, pushed around, lied to, misled, and manipulated. Tired of Kelso, the cowboy act, the stubborn brawn.

He couldn't justify hanging around here much longer, but neither did he have to leave in a big hurry just because he'd been ordered to. Tamara wasn't expecting him at the agency until Wednesday morning; he didn't need to be on the road until this time tomorrow night. Kelso's ultimatum didn't concern him. There was no basis for an obstruction charge no matter how many locals he talked to.

He was beginning to see the shape of what was going on in Gray's Landing. Keep asking the right questions, make the right connections, and the focus would sharpen. If he saw it clear enough over the next twenty-four hours, he'd give it to Joe Rinniak before he left for San Francisco.

18

TAMARA

Cold, fog-drippy morning. Past few days hadn't been too bad, but now your standard San Francisco summer weather was back again. Well, all that gray matched her mood. Fallout from Vonda's little bombshell last night. Just what she needed—something new to rock her world.

She was first at the agency, as usual. Turned up the heat to get rid of the damp chill, made a pot of coffee . . . damn glorified secretary. Booted up her Mac and checked e-mail until the coffee was ready. Since she'd lost the twenty pounds, she drank it black; this morning she dumped in two packets of dairy creamer and a teaspoonful of sugar. She'd hate herself for it later, but right now she didn't care.

She sat sipping the sweetened coffee and staring at the blank computer screen. Why did she feel so down anyway? Vonda'd been her best friend since high school.

Shared all kinds of confidences, even the gory details when each of them lost their viriginity. Two of a kind, weren't they? Wild childs with chips on their shoulders, dissing Whitey, smoking dope, drinking wine, hanging and banging with the bad boys. Vowing they'd always be outlaws. None of the conventional crap for them. Husbands, families—forget it. Get gobbled up by Whitey's world like her sister, Claudia—no way. Only trouble with that 'tude was, if you were smart and your old man was a cop and Vonda's was a fireman and both of you grew up a long way from the ghetto and had never even tasted poverty, you couldn't keep the chips from sliding off eventually. Things happened. You got older; you found out you had computer skills or an interest in interior design; you decided you might as well give college a try; you met somebody who was smart and talented and had never had a chip; you needed extra money so you drifted into jobs like this one or a sales position at the S.F. Design Center. And the next thing you knew, the hard edge was gone and you were an adult with adult responsibilities; you had career ambitions that were rooted smack in the middle of a world that maybe wasn't so much Whitey's anymore after all.

Tamara had always figured that if either of them was going to throw off her teenage rebellion and settle down to marriage and kids, it would be her. Her and Horace. Not Vonda. That girl liked men too much. Different men, as long as they were black. No home and hearth bullshit for her. How many times had Vonda said that over the years? But things kept happening on that front, too. Horace moving to Philly and taking up with Mary from Rochester, and Vonda meeting a suit who worked in a Financial District brokerage house, a suit who happened to be both white *and* Jewish, and falling in love with him like she'd fallen in love with fifty other guys she'd been to bed with except that this time, for some weird reason, it was the real thing. And then she shows up at the apartment last night, no warning, so excited she looks like she's about to pop, and drops her bombshell.

Pregnant.

Getting married right away.

And the weird thing was, Tamara wasn't sure which of the two tweaked her the most.

Didn't have anything to do with Ben Sherman's color or religion, though both were going to be a problem for Vonda. One of her brothers was a dead-bang racist; already been some friction, and he'd go ballistic when he found out. Vonda didn't care about that, at least not right now, so why should she? No, what was bugging her was something more personal. She knew what it was. Might as well admit it to herself.

Jealous. Stupid, but there it was. Jealous on both counts.

Horace, the love of her life, gone for good. She didn't have anybody now, not even a casual bed partner. And Vonda was not only getting married to the love of *her* life, so she claimed; she was also pleased and happy about the life growing inside her, the family she'd sworn she'd never have. Wanted that baby, all right, dirty diapers and 3:00 A.M. feedings and all the rest of it. Ought to be grateful it wasn't *her* who was knocked up, but instead, here she was turning a couple of pale shades of green over a girlfriend who was facing all kinds of mixed-marriage wife and mother problems.

Why would she *want* to be saddled with a kid of her own at this stage, with her career on the rise and her time already at a premium? She didn't, not really. And yet . . . she kept thinking about that scared little kidnapped girl, Lauren, and the way the two of them had bonded during the long hours they'd been held captive together five months ago. Brought out all sorts of maternal instincts she hadn't even known she had. Made her pine a little then, and now and then since, for her own kid someday. She'd make a good mother, no question about that. Good wife, too. Well, she'd have a chance to find out someday, wouldn't she? Probably. Sure. She was only twenty-six. Plenty of time.

Someday.

Angrily, the anger directed inward, she forced herself to get to work. Balm for everything, work. Frustration, yearning, sexual need, maternity, loneliness . . . just throw yourself into your job, let it take over your mind, and all of the bad got pushed far enough aside so you could forget it was there. For a while, anyway.

She was deep into the background search on Anthony Drax when Bill came in carrying a white gift box. *He* was in a good mood, at least. Looked like he'd had a good night's sleep. Looked like the cancer scare was going to turn out all right, thank God. Kerry was a survivor and so was he; they had each other, that was how they'd been able to get through the strain and pain of the past three months. You could get through just about anything if you had somebody to hang on to, somebody who cared enough to be there for you . . .

And here we go again and the hell with that.

She put on a smiley face for him so he wouldn't start asking personal questions. "How'd it go with Mathias yesterday?"

"He's a piece of work, all right. Everything Celeste Ogden said he was."

"You meet Dracula?"

"Unfortunately. Birds of a feather, the two of them."

"Bats."

"What?"

"Bats of a wing."

Pretty feeble, but he chuckled anyway. Only lame thing about Bill was that he didn't have much of a sense of humor and what he did have was conventional. Hers was off-the-wall; Horace had told her once that she ought to do stand-up. Yeah, well. You could put Bill on without half-trying. She'd done it so often and so wickedly on occasion that sometimes she felt ashamed afterward.

She listened while he recounted his interviews with Mathias and Drax and with Mathias's neighbor and Philomena Ruiz. Interesting. Couple of things that needed to be checked out. First one was that silver sports car the neighbor woman had seen. As deep as Tamara had gone on both Mathias and Drax, it hadn't seemed necessary to find out what kinds of cars they drove. Now it did, and never mind that Mathias had apparently been in Chicago the night his wife died.

Bill tapped the gift box, which he'd set down on her desk. "Nancy Mathias's records," he said. "I went through the receipts again last night. I didn't make the connection before, but two of the paid bills came from a Dr. Robert J. Prince. Doesn't say what his specialty is—he's part of a Geary Street consortium called Medical Associates, Inc. Neurologist, probably. There's also a bill for diagnostic tests at U.C. Med Center."

"Check that out, too."

"You might want to go through the records yourself. I don't think Kerry and I missed anything, but you never know. I'd like to take a look at the last six months of her diary entries, same reason. Can you e-mail them to Kerry's computer when you get the chance?"

"No problem."

"You find out anything new on Mathias?"

"No. Man's background is so clean it shines. Got to be some dirt somewhere—nobody's that perfect—but he's got himself covered every way there is."

"How about Drax? You do him yet?"

"Working on him when you came in. Same thing so far. Graduate of Cal Poly with honors and a degree in computer science. Worked in Silicon Valley for ten years before he went to RingTech—two big E companies, moving on up the corporate ladder. Another success-at-any-cost type, probably unscrupulous as hell but nothing to prove it. No felony record, no misdeameanor record, no known underworld connections. Never been married. Been living with a Delta stewardess named Donna Lane in Atherton for the past six months."

"He's protective of Mathias," Bill said. "Looks up to him, probably envies him. Considers him a genius, a Forbes list mover and shaker. I can see him doing just about anything Mathias asked of him if he were promised a piece of the action."

"Like killing his wife."

"But it still comes down to motive. Why would Mathias want his wife dead badly enough to recruit Drax for the dirty work? Drax or anybody else? That's the sticking point."

Tamara didn't get back to work right away. After Bill retreated to his office, she went out and refilled her coffee cup and stood at the front windows for a couple of minutes, looking down at the empty South Park playground below. Her mood had shifted. Different perspective now, the self-critical kind.

You know what you are, girl? she thought. You're a fool. One of those it's-all-about-me fools.

Part of the mood shift had come from thinking about how putting Bill on made her feel ashamed sometimes. Wasn't the only thing she had to be ashamed about. Mooning around, pity partying, because her best friend was pregant and getting married and she didn't have a man of her own anymore and motherhood was a long way off. So Horace was gone and she didn't have a love life right now, so what? She was still one lucky black woman, come right down to it. Look at all the brothers and sisters living in the projects and the ghettos in Visitacion Valley and Hunters Point and East Oakland, all the poverty, all the drugs, all the zoned-out gangbangers with automatic weapons, all the innocent people who died every day for no sane reason. She wasn't caught in that trap, never would be. She had a job she loved, goals that could be reached. Lived pretty well right now and her future prospects were even better. Most important, she was in a position to help people in trouble, right some wrongs, see some justice done.

More she could do on that score, too—a lot more. Such as take on pro bono cases for African-Americans and Latinos and other ethnics in trouble who needed the agency's services but couldn't afford them.

It wasn't an inspiration; she'd considered the idea before. Just hadn't done anything about it because of how busy they were. Yeah, right. Lame excuse. You can find time for anything if you care about it enough. And she did care. Always had, always would.

All right. Talk to Bill about it, first opportunity. He'd be for it; man was color-blind and dripped milk of human kindness. Might mean hiring another investigator and an office manager, take some of the burden off the two of them and Jake and Alex Chavez. It'd cut their profit margin, but that didn't matter. Doing something, making a difference—that mattered.

And meanwhile, no more playing the it's-all-about-me game. She'd been a little short and unsympathetic with Vonda last night. Call her tonight, go see her, make it right. You weren't good to your friends and family, didn't keep them close, you really would end up alone—you'd die alone, sad and bitter and desperate, the way Nancy Mathias had.

Tamara went back to her desk feeling better.

The sports car lead took a while to track, because of the laws that prevented easy access to DMV records. Turned out Mathias had two cars registered in his name, a Lexus and a Lincoln Continental. Drax owned a Mercedes sedan. The woman Drax was living with? Something there, maybe: Donna Lane drove a three-year-old BMW Z3. Sports car, but the color wasn't listed. She could find out, only it would take some time.

Dr. Robert J. Prince first. Figured to be a routine follow-up, but it wasn't. When she found out his specialty, it surprised her enough to put in a phone call to the Medical Associates offices on Geary. Dr. Prince was "unavailable," whatever that meant. She tried the need-to-know-for-insurance-purposes dodge with his nurse, but that didn't get her anywhere. Under no circumstances, the nurse said crisply, did Dr. Prince give out information about his patients, alive or deceased.

She went across into Bill's office. "Got something," she said.

"The sports car?"

"Nancy Mathias. Her headaches weren't simple migraines after all."

"No?"

"Dr. Robert Prince isn't a neurologist. He's a specialist in intercranial disorders—a brain surgeon."

19

JAKE RUNYON

He was waiting when Sandra Parnell arrived for work at the Hair Today Salon on Tuesday morning.

He'd tried to see her the night before—twice. Nobody home the first time he went to her house, around six. Her father answered the door the second time, a little after eight—a dull, vague man in his fifties who smelled of cheap whiskey and wore the bewildered look of an Alzheimer's patient. He had no idea where Sandra was, or what time she'd be home. "She's not in any more trouble, is she?" he said, but not as if he cared much.

The salon was on a side street on the eastern edge of downtown, a narrow storefront sandwiched between a *tacqueria* and a defunct bookstore. A sign on the door gave the opening time as 9:30. Runyon drove around the corner and through an alley that bisected the block. There was a rear entrance but no parking facilities back there. He circled around again, parked, and waited near the front entrance.

Sandra Parnell's old Chrysler came up the street at 9:25, slid into a space near the corner. Part of her job must be to open up in the morning; nobody'd gone into the salon before her. She didn't notice him as she walked back. Eyes front all the way. He stayed put until she was at the door fumbling with her keys, then got out quickly and approached her just as she got it open.

"Hello, Sandra."

She blinked at him, startled. "Oh—Mr. Runyon. You're still here."

"Talk to you for a minute?"

"Well, I've got to get things ready inside—"

"We can talk while you're doing it. I won't keep you long."

She hesitated, gnawed at her lip, said, "All right," and went on in. He trailed after her as she turned the CLOSED sign around and then went to put on the lights. Small place, four chairs in four open cubicles. Clean and neat enough, but with a faintly shabby aura. The sweetish chemical smell of hair lotions and conditioners was thick on the dead air.

She said, "I haven't heard from Jerry. I keep hoping, but . . . not a word."

"What would you have done if you had?"

"I . . . don't know. After Sunday and Deputy Kelso, and then the fire at the camp . . . I just don't know."

"Kelso give you a hard time?"

"Kind of. At the station and then in front of my parents. He wouldn't believe I don't know where Jerry is."

"Any possibilities occur to you?"

"No. If they had, I'd've gone to look."

"You still love him, then."

"Sure I do. Why'd you ask that?"

"And he loves you."

"I thought he did, until he ran away from the camp."

"How long have you been going with him?"

"About seven months."

"No problems between you in that time?"

"Problems?"

"Arguments, harsh words."

"No."

"He ever hit you for any reason?"

She stopped arranging combs, scissors, other things, in one of the cubicles. "Hit me? Jerry?"

"Ashley Kelso says he could be violent."

"Not violent exactly, just . . . rough sometimes."

"Then he did hit you."

"Not hard, not trying to hurt me."

"Not even when he was high?"

"No. Ashley told you he beat her up, didn't she? That's what she told her father Jerry did to her. Kelso tried to get me to say Jerry beat me up, too, but I wouldn't because it's not true."

"Not true in Ashley's case, either?"

"She never said anything to me. I don't believe it."

"Why would she make it up?"

"Because she's pissed at Jerry for dumping her and going with me."

"Jealous?"

"No. She doesn't blame me, she blames Jerry."

"So you're not still friends."

"Not really, not anymore."

"Why did Jerry dump you, Sandra?"

"What?" Shocked look. "He didn't dump me. Did Ashley tell you that?"

"No. Jerry's folks."

"It's not true. Why would they say that?"

"Three weeks ago. Because he found out something about you."

"Found out what?"

"Secrets, Sandra? Something you were hiding from him?"

"No! I never hid anything from Jerry, I told him everything. He didn't dump me three weeks ago or any time. I love him and he loves me. We're going to get married someday—we are!"

Runyon said nothing. The girl looked him straight in the eye, her expression earnest despite the evidence of strain.

"Don't you believe me?" she said.

Battle Hardware was the old-fashioned kind of hardware store—narrow aisles, crowded shelves, bins full of nails and screws and the like, rough wooden floors that retained the faint smell of creosote. There were no customers when Runyon walked in, just one elderly employee perched on a stool behind the counter and the lanky kid with the mop of caramel-colored hair restocking shelves of plumbing supplies.

Zach Battle recognized him. "Oh . . . hi," he said with neither enthusiasm nor hostility. "Mr. Runyon, right?"

"Right. Your father around?"

"No. He's at city hall this morning."

"Mayor's office?"

"Yeah. Until one o'clock."

"Talk to you for a minute?"

"What about?"

"What everybody's talking about in Gray's Landing."

"I don't know anything about those fires."

"No opinions, no ideas?"

"It's none of my business."

"Friend of Jerry Belsize's, aren't you?"

"Not really. He does his thing, I do mine."

"Ashley Kelso have anything to do with why you don't get along?"

"I don't have to answer that."

"That's right, you don't. You think Jerry's guilty?"

"If he is, I hope they lock him up for the rest of his life."

"Doesn't answer my question."

"You don't have any right to ask me questions. You're not the law here; you don't even live in this county."

"Why should you mind talking to me?"

"I don't mind. I just don't have anything to say. About Belsize or the fires or any of the rest of it."

"Your father tell you to keep quiet?"

"No."

"Deputy Kelso?"

"No. Nobody tells me what to do."

"Not even Ashley?"

The kid didn't like that. "Why don't you go talk to my dad?" he said as if he was issuing a challenge. "He likes to talk. I don't."

The Gray's Landing city hall sat on a block-square rise on the other side of the park from the sheriff's substation. Gray stone edifice built in the twenties in the neoclassical style of public buildings of that era. If there'd been any renovations done since, the work wasn't obvious either outside or inside. It had a semideserted aspect, as if the town in general had lost interest in the place and the day when it would shut its doors permanently wasn't far off.

The mayor's office was on the second floor front. Carl Battle was there, and he didn't keep Runyon waiting when an elderly secretary announced him. Battle came around from behind an old mahogany desk set in front of a brace of open windows, clasped his hand, all but guided him into one of a pair of thinly padded visitors' chairs. Deferential, ill at ease. He wore the same suit and tie as on their last meeting, or ones just like them, and his balding head was just as sweaty, his handshake just as damp and limp. It was stuffy in the small private office. No breeze came in through the open windows, and a ceiling fan stirred the air without cooling it any.

"Thank you for stopping by, Mr. Runyon," he said. "Much appreciated. Ah, how's your head?"

"Still sore."

"Of course. But no serious aftereffects, I trust?"

"No."

"Good, good." Battle cleared his throat before he said, "Ah, about your medical costs. You remember I suggested the county might pay for them? Well, I spoke to several officials, but—"

"Don't worry about it. My insurance will take care of most of it."

"Good, good," Battle said again, sounding relieved. "I imagine you're eager to be back in San Francisco."

"Eager enough."

"When will you be leaving?"

"Today."

"Today, yes, I thought you would be." He went around behind his desk, sat down heavily. "Difficult times," he said vaguely. "Very difficult."

Runyon was silent.

"We've been overrun with the media, but I suppose you know that. Have they bothered you?"

"I've had a couple of calls."

"Talked to any of them yet?"

"No."

"Do you plan to?"

"Not if I can avoid it."

"I don't blame you a bit. Vultures, the lot of them." He produced a handkerchief, mopped his face. "I wish to

234 • Bill Pronzini

heaven we could afford air-conditioning. Summer days like this, it's an oven in here by mid-afternoon. But we're not a well-off community, much as I hate to admit it. Just don't have the money in the city coffers to pay for everything we need, even some of the basics. Have to make do with what we have and what we can afford."

Prepared speech. You could tell by Battle's delivery and the way his golf ball–sized Adam's apple bobbed above the knot in his tie. Runyon knew what it was leading into. Subtlety wasn't one of the mayor's long suits.

"Gray's Landing used to be prosperous, you know," Battle said. He mopped his face again. Sweat beads glistened on the top of his head, but he seemed not to be bothered by those. "Agriculture is our lifeblood. There was a time when there were dozens of prosperous farms in the area, hundreds of acres of fruit and olive orchards, two packing plants that employed more than two hundred people. But times have been lean in recent years. Very lean. First RipeOlive Processors in Stander went to a skeleton crew, then out of business, and right after that Westridge Produce closed its doors. Lost jobs, stores closing downtown, lost city revenue . . . I'm sure you understand the negative effects on a small community like ours."

Runyon nodded, listening and not listening.

"And now these terrible arson fires . . . the murder of a prominent Latino . . . all the publicity. It has everyone on edge. Frightened, worried. Not themselves. There's tremendous pressure on public officials like myself, like

Deputy Kelso, to put an end to it before the community is so severely damaged it may never recover."

Battle worked the handkerchief again, watching him over the top of it. Runyon still had nothing to say.

"Good people, Mr. Runyon. John Belsize and his wife; Don Kelso. Good people under extreme pressure." Rambling a little now. "You shouldn't judge them too harshly."

"I don't judge them at all."

"Good, good. I know the deputy has been a little rough on you, but I hope you won't hold it against him. His job . . . well, it takes its toll on a man. Shortens his temper, makes him seem more severe than he really is. Well, you see what I mean."

"You don't have to worry about that, either, Mayor."

"About . . . what?"

"I'm not going to make trouble for Kelso, or the Belsizes, or you, or Gray's Landing. No public denouncements, no reports of harassment, no personal injury lawsuit."

Battle said hastily, "Oh, well, I never thought—"

"Sure you did. But you can put your mind at rest. I'm not vindictive and I'm not litigious. And I want to see the person responsible for the crimes caught as much as you or anyone else."

"Yes, yes, of course you do."

"So now we understand each other."

"Yes. Perfectly. I . . . well . . ."

"That's all that needs to be said."

Battle gave him a weak smile, used the handkerchief

again—blotted the top of his head with it this time. When Runyon stood up, Battle said, "Thank you, Mr. Runyon. If there's ever anything I can do . . ."

"As a matter of fact, there's something you can do right now." The label fragment he'd found in the migrant camp trailer was in his wallet; he took it out, laid it on the desk. "Recognize this?"

The mayor squinted at it. "Why, yes. It's one of Ripe-Olive's labels."

"RipeOlive. The processing plant that went out of business last year."

"That's right. After forty years. They just couldn't compete any—"

"You said they went to a skeleton crew before they shut down. Who headed the crew?"

"I believe it was Martin Parnell. Why?"

"Where was it RipeOlive was located? Spander?"

"No, Stander. Five miles south of here, off the frontage road."

"Many of these labels still around?"

"I suppose so," Battle said. He turned the fragment over. "On jars and bottles. But this one doesn't appear to have been used. The glue's still smooth. How did you come by it?"

Runyon said, "Found it stuck to a shoe," and retrieved the fragment and put it back into his wallet. Another of the mayor's sweaty handshakes and a few more murmurs of civic gratitude, and he was out of there.

•   •   •

In the shade of a locust tree on the city hall lawn, he used his cell phone to put in a long-distance call to the agency in San Francisco. He was pretty sure, now, that he knew what had tweaked his memory when he first picked up the label fragment, but he needed to be certain. He asked Tamara to pull up the file on his routine background check on Gerald Belsize, read him the list of full- and part-time jobs the kid had held since his high-school graduation.

Right. Number two was summer grunt work at Ripe-Olive Processors three years ago.

20

FIREBUG

"Tonight. We'll do it tonight."

"Can't we wait a little longer, make sure?"

"We've waited long enough."

"What if he's not—"

"How many times do I have to tell you? It doesn't matter."

"It matters to me."

"Stop whining! I hate it when you do that."

"I'm sorry, I can't help thinking—"

"You want me to smack you?"

"No."

"Then don't argue with me. We'll do it just like we planned."

"What about Runyon?"

"Forget about him, will you? He's doesn't know any-thing."

"Are you sure?"

"Yes, yes, I'm sure."

". . . All right. Whatever you say."

"I'm so amped I don't want to wait until tonight—I want to do it right *now*."

"God, no, not in the daytime."

"I'm just saying I want to."

"But we're not going to until tonight."

"Fire's better at night. Brighter, hotter."

"Yes."

"It's what we both want."

"Yes."

"Payback."

"Yes."

And the flames, the burning.

"Are we going in and . . . you know, check first?"

"We have to. We can't leave any traces."

"I don't think I can stand it."

"You'll stand it, all right. If I can, you can."

"I'll probably puke."

"Then go ahead and puke. I'm gonna laugh. I'm laugh-ing right now."

"I don't think I'll ever laugh again."

"There you go again. Candy ass! Just shut up and do what I tell you, or I swear I'll make you sorry."

"Don't get mad."

"I'm not mad. Amped, totally amped."

"Can I ask you one thing? Then I won't say another word."

"Well?"

"Promise me this'll be the last time?"

"Last time for what?"

"Fires."

"What else?"

"Games."

"What else?"

"Payback."

"What else?"

"You know."

"I don't know. What else?"

"Killing. I don't want to kill any more people; I don't want you to. Please? For me?"

"All right. For you."

But only for a while. A very short while.

So much more to burn, so much more to pay back.

The biggest, the hottest, the best, was yet to come.

21

When I arrived at the medical building at 450 Geary, Celeste Ogden was waiting for me in the lobby. Two-oh-five by my watch, which made me ten minutes early; she'd been there since quarter till, she said. She didn't look anxious, but neither was she as imperious as usual. Willfully self-contained, like a businesswoman about to take a difficult and probably unpleasant meeting, whatever she was thinking or feeling hidden behind a controlled facade. I liked her better that way; it made her seem more human.

She was the reason we were both here. She and her vascular surgeon husband, Arnold Ogden. There was no way on earth Tamara or I could have induced Dr. Robert J. Prince to grant an audience, much less breach patient–doctor confidentiality even though the patient was deceased, but one phone call to Celeste Ogden, another from her to her husband, a third from the esteemed Dr. Ogden to his colleague. Dr. Prince was scheduled for office consultations this afternoon, fortunately; he'd agreed to squeeze us in for a few minutes at 2:15.

I had a pretty good idea of what we were going to find out from Dr. Prince, and I think Celeste Ogden did, too. We hadn't discussed it; time enough for that afterward. We rode the elevator up to the twelfth floor in silence.

Dr. Robert J. Prince's name headed the list of six on the door to Medical Associates' large, plush suite of offices. Prominent big-money physicians all, and no doubt worth what they earned. These offices were mainly for consultations and record keeping, I gathered. The doctors would spend most of their time at U.C. Med Center, S.F. General, and whatever hospitals in the Bay Area required their specialty services.

We were shown into Dr. Prince's office promptly at 2:15. He greeted us politely but with restraint and reluctance. African-American, about my age, his graying hair close cropped, his manner unprepossessing. Deep, soft voice. Large hands, the fingers very long and supple. He had a habit of flexing them in different small ways, as if he were engaging in a series of private aerobic exercises.

When we were all seated he said to Celeste Ogden, "I have great respect for your husband, Mrs. Ogden. He's a fine surgeon and I consider him a friend."

"He feels the same about you."

"I'm glad to hear it. But the point is, I've agreed to this meeting only as a favor to him and with no little reluctance. Patient confidentiality is a very important part of my practice. I wouldn't have agreed if your sister was still alive."

"Yes, we understand that."

"So before we begin, I must ask you not to repeat to anyone what is said here today."

I nodded, but she said, "Agreed, unless the information becomes relevant in a criminal case."

"What sort of criminal case?"

"Homicide."

"I don't see how that's possible."

"It may not be," I said. "We don't know yet."

"If it is," Celeste Ogden said, "would you be willing to testify in court? In the interest of justice?"

He thought that over. At length he said carefully, "I am always willing to further the cause of justice."

"Thank you, Doctor."

"Ask your questions," he said.

My job. "When did Nancy Mathias first come to you?"

"A little over a month ago."

"Referred by?"

"Her physician in Palo Alto, Dr. Koslowski. She was suffering from what she believed were increasingly serious migraine headaches. Additional symptoms—nausea and vomiting, vision difficulties, increasing weakness on the left side of her body—were such that he ordered tests which proved that the condition was much more serious."

"What was the condition?"

"Anaplastic malignant ependymoma."

"In layman's terms, Doctor?"

"A brain tumor," he said.

"Operable?"

"Inoperable, because of its location. Radiation was the only viable option, and a poor one in her case."

"It wouldn't have cured her?"

"Saved her life, you mean? No. The tumor was malignant and fast growing."

"How long did she have?"

"A year, at the most."

"At the least?"

"Perhaps six months."

Well, there it was. The explanation for the August diary entries, the reason Nancy had given the $10,000 to T. R. Quentin and refused to take any of the woman's paintings. It opened up other possibilities, too. I glanced at Celeste Ogden. She hadn't moved or changed expression. Will of iron, I thought.

"You told this to Mrs. Mathias, of course."

"Of course," Dr. Prince said. "I must say she took it bravely."

"When was this?"

He consulted a paper on his desk. "August twenty-second. The day after I received the final test results."

"Here in your office?"

"Yes."

"Did she come alone, or with her husband?"

"Alone. I understood Mr. Mathias was to be present, but he didn't come."

"Did he join her on subsequent visits?"

"He did not."

"Did he ever contact you about his wife's condition or prognosis?"

"No."

"Did you try to contact him?"

"No. Mrs. Mathias asked me not to."

"Did she say why?"

"Only that she would tell him when the time came. She didn't want anyone else to know."

"Not even me," Celeste Ogden said.

"I'm sorry, Mrs. Ogden. Not even you."

That son of a bitch!" she said. Her first words since we'd left the Medical Associates offices. Low, hard, venomous. Mathias, of course, not Dr. Prince.

We were alone in the elevator going down. She stood with her back tight to one wall, staring straight ahead. There were cracks in the armored facade now, a moist sheen to her eyes. This was as close as she would ever come, I thought, to a public display of emotion.

"He didn't care enough to be there for her, even after she told him. She did tell him; her diary proves that."

"Yes."

"I hate him," she said. "God, I've never hated anyone as much as I hate that man."

"You have good reason."

So did I, for that matter, whether he was guilty of complicity in his wife's death or not. There was a disturbing, close-to-home parallel here. Nancy Mathias had had a malignant tumor; so had Kerry. One inoperable, prognosis negative; one operable, prognosis favorable. And Mathias's reaction when he was given the grim verdict? Unresponsive, nonsupportive, even argumentative. He couldn't have loved his wife, or cared about what she was going through, the turmoil of fear and suffering. Kerry was life itself to me. How could I not hate that kind of man, that kind of selfish indifference? Oh yeah. As much as you can hate a virtual stranger.

The elevator doors whispered open and we started across the lobby. Mrs. Ogden murmured, more to herself than to me, "Why didn't Nancy want me to know? Him, yes, but not me? I loved her, I'd have done anything for her. She knew that."

Rhetorical question. The kind answer was that Nancy hadn't wanted to upset her; the probable truth was that Mathias's control was too strong and he wouldn't allow it. She'd told him, all right, two days after she found out on August 22. The following week he'd again promised to meet her at Dr. Prince's and then failed to show up, using an important meeting as an excuse; that was what her angry diary entry that week referred to. The handwritten note among her papers was another unanswered plea for his presence at a consultation with Dr. Prince. "D," in her shorthand, stood for doctor.

Outside on the sidewalk, Mrs. Ogden said, "I was wrong."

"Wrong about what?"

"As miserable as he is, as much as I loathe him, he couldn't have been responsible for Nancy's death. It must have been a tragic accident after all."

"What makes you say that?"

"If she was dying, with less than a year to live, there's no reason for him to have had her killed, is there?"

"Mercy killing, put an early end to her suffering," I said, but I didn't believe it.

Neither did she. "There's no mercy in him. Not an ounce."

I could see one other motive, now, given the kind of man Mathias was—the most monstrous, obscene motive for spousal homicide imaginable. It started my blood boiling just thinking about it. But I kept it to myself. Conjecture, with nothing to back it up. And that was what I'd been concerned about all along, the source of the bad feeling about this investigation.

How the hell could murder be proven, by me or anybody else?

22

She didn't know what to do with herself.

For a while she worked on her computer, but there just wasn't much for her to do from home. It was make-work anyway. Jim Carpenter and Miranda Doyle were covering her accounts; she gave them input on concepts, copy, art, TV and radio spots, but time pressures meant that they were the ones responsible for most of the creative refinements and for organizing the campaigns. What she was given was already-completed work for her rubber-stamp approval. Her function since she'd taken the leave of absence was mainly advisory.

She read a couple more chapters in *The Magic Island*. Interesting enough, if a stretch of credulity, but her mind kept wandering. Hyperactive lately, thoughts and ideas piling up, tumbling against one another. Part of it was cabin fever. But it was more than that, too. She had already broken through the shell of fear and anxiety she'd been trapped in for the past three months. The medical ordeal was finished; the tumor and the cancerous cells were gone; the prognosis was favorable. She felt fine aside from the soreness and stiffness from the radiation burning, and even that wasn't nearly as bad as it had been during the last few treatments. Her stamina was coming back; she didn't need daily naps anymore; she was sleeping well and had energy most of the time. Her sex drive hadn't quite returned, but the fact that she was thinking about it again, and had discussed it with Bill, meant that it was only a matter of time. Lovemaking, for a while, might not be very pleasant; there was bound to be some awkwardness and probably some discomfort. But that wasn't going to prevent her from doing it. For her own sake as well as his.

Next week sometime. And next week she would be back at Bates and Carpenter full-time—resume that important part of her life as well. She'd already talked to Jim Carpenter about it. He was just as eager for her return as she was.

Bill thought it was premature. He felt she ought to stay home another couple of weeks, rest, continue to build up her strength. He'd been a rock throughout this damn crisis, she couldn't have gotten through it as well as she had without him, but he couldn't seem to let go of his concern for her. He was still afraid, and she loved him even more for that, but you can't keep existing in a constant state of anxiety and fear. She wasn't any longer. She couldn't say exactly when she'd emerged, but it had been before the end of the radiation therapy. Woke up one morning and she was no longer afraid—fear today, gone tomorrow. In its place was the growing, driving need for normalcy, to be in control of her life again, to be whole and live whole. He said he understood how she felt, but he didn't, really. You had to experience it to understand it fully. And please, God, don't ever put *him* in that position.

Thinking about him made her feel tender. He was so many things, most of them good, a few bemusing, one or two annoying. Like all men, she supposed. He probably felt the same about her, about all women. Women are from Venus; men are from Mars—true enough. She still hadn't quite forgiven him for keeping the knowledge of Cybil's wartime rape from her, or the now-disproven possibility that that bastard Russ Dancer and not Ivan Wade was her father. Hadn't quite forgiven Cybil, either, for that matter, though she could understand her mother's need to keep the secret all these years. The woman thing again. But she'd never been able to stay angry at Bill for long. Even if he wasn't justified in circumventing her right to know, he'd done it for the same basic reason Cybil had—to protect her because he loved her, didn't want to see her hurt. You couldn't really fault him for that. Part of what made him a good husband, wasn't it? Part of what made a good marriage. Caring combined with love, desire, friendship, understanding, a little mystery, and spiced with a clash of wills and attitudes every now and then. By those standards, theirs was just about the best you could ask for.

It was after one now and she still hadn't had lunch. She'd thought about going out to eat, driving over to Larkspur and taking Cybil out or calling Paula to see if she was free. But she wasn't quite up to a long solitary drive yet or in a mood for Paula and her new voodoo passion, and the prospect of a restaurant meal alone didn't appeal to her, either. She made herself a green salad with tomatoes and avocado and strips of leftover chicken. While she ate, she considered her options for the rest of the afternoon.

Too restless to sit around here. She needed to get out somewhere for a while. A walk in Golden Gate Park would be nice, but it was foggy and cold again today and even if she bundled up, it probably wasn't a wise idea. No, but she could still go to the park—visit the de Young. She hadn't been in some time, since shortly after the museum's architecturally controversial new home had opened. She'd enjoyed the visit to Brookline Gallery on Sunday, the exhibit of T. R. Quentin's paintings, but as good as Quentin's work was, it was neither fine art nor as stimulating.

Settled. Check her e-mail again on the slim chance that something pressing had come in from the agency, and then she was out of here.

Shameless followed her into the spare bedroom, hopped up on her desk, and peered at the screen as if he were also trying to read her messages. Nosy animal, but good company just the same. Nothing from Jim or Miranda or anyone else at Bates and Carpenter. But there was one e-mail of interest, from Tamara, sent at Bill's request: Nancy

Mathias's diary entries over the last six months of her life. Tamara had picked out the ones that struck her as meaningful, but he probably wanted to have a look at the entire batch himself. Even as technologically challenged as he was, he could manage to open a computer file and scan through the contents.

So could she, with a lot more ease.

Better not. The idea of peering at a dead woman's private thoughts still struck Kerry as ghoulish. And she and Bill had always been respectful of each other's privacy—no interference in personal or professional business matters. Then again, they had no secrets from each other, and he'd let her go through Nancy Mathias's private papers with him, hadn't he? Involved her in the investigation? And last night, before they went to bed and without her asking, he'd volunteered a full report on his meetings with Brandon Mathias and Anthony Drax, what he'd learned from the elderly neighbor in Palo Alto and from Philomena Ruiz. No earthly reason why he'd object to her looking at the diary entries.

Oh, hell, go ahead, she thought. It may be ghoulish, but you can't help being curious. Or wanting to play detective.

She opened the file and began to read.

Painful experience. She'd been prepared for it, or thought she was, but a linear paging through day after day of loneliness, misery, and reported abuses by the son of a bitch Nancy Mathias had married was not the same as being presented with a capsule summary. Poor woman. Some of her suffering had been brought on by her own weakness, her inability to walk away from that hellish relationship. But she'd been under tremendous psychological pressure and it's not always easy to know what to do under those circumstances. Control freak Mathias was responsible for most of her pain, yet it was clear that something else, some other force, was affecting her as well. Did that force, whatever it was, have anything to do with her murder? If it was murder. Tamara was right: there was nothing in the diary entries, no matter how you looked at them, that suggested a motive.

Kerry read to the final entry, sighed, and looked at the time in the upper corner of the screen. Already 1:30; she'd better hustle over to the de Young before it got any later.

She started to close the file so she could shut down. And stopped herself, frowning, staring at the screen. The final entry stared back at her.

Time. Date and time.

September 9, 10:05 P.M.
WHY ADHERE?

Something there that didn't seem quite right . . .
Yes, it did. *Now* it did.
Of course!
Excited, she picked up the phone and called Bill's cell.

23

JAKE RUNYON

Stander was a nowhere place.

Not a village or a hamlet—an old, disused railroad siding. If it had ever been anything more, the only evidence left standing were a gutted stone building between the two-lane blacktop and the main rail line, the remains of a water tank, and the fenced-in compound that had once been RipeOlive Processors. Nearest signs of life were a farmhouse some distance back, a combination country store and junk dealer a quarter of a mile before that. Anybody's guess who or what Stander had been, or why the siding had a name at all.

Olive groves stretched out on both sides of the road here, flanking the compound to the east, hiding Highway 5 to the west. Some of the gnarled trees looked as though they were still being harvested; others seemed as dead as the RipeOlive buildings. The plant was set back a hundred yards or so from the blacktop, the chain-link fence around it and the entrance gates capped by slanted strands of barbed wire. The main rail line was still in service—the condition of the rails and ties told you that—but the spur that branched off to the plant, weed choked, broken up, rusty, hadn't been used in years.

Runyon turned off onto a potholed ribbon of pavement that bent up across the right-of-way. The paved portion of the road looped around to the front gates; a once-graveled, now mostly dirt track intersected it near the fence corner, led around to the olive groves at the rear. On a pole next to the gates stood a metal sign, bullet pocked where somebody had used it for target practice, the green and black lettering on it beginning to fade:

RipeOlive Brand
"From Our Trees to Your Table"

Two buildings, both of unpainted wood with sheet-metal roofs, were visible inside the fence from here—a long, low warehouse and a shorter structure that formed a detached ell on the north side. Coming in, he'd seen a third building at the rear, some kind of long shed stretched out parallel to the warehouse. The yard was paved, the pavement cracking and sprouting weeds and dry grass. Heat shimmered over everything, gave the buildings an insubstantial, two-dimensional look.

Just what he'd expected to find.

Nowhere place, abandoned place.

He got out to examine the gates. Double padlocked, the locks showing rust and free of key scrapes. No signs of life in the compound, or that anybody had been in there recently—not from this vantage point. Another entrance?

Back in the car, he U-turned to the dirt road and followed it along the side fence. Thin plumes of dust rose up behind, seemed to hang in the sultry air before they began to settle. The fence, as far as he could tell, hadn't been breached anywhere on this side or at the rear.

The road split again back there, one branch veering in among the trees, the other continuing parallel to the fence. Two-thirds of the way along the latter he came on another, smaller set of gates. Rear entrance for trucks coming in from the groves. He stopped there and went over for a look. Padlocked, like the main entrance, but when he tugged on the lock it came open: the shackle had been set into the case, so that it seemed secure at a glance, but it hadn't been pressed down to engage the locking mechanism. On the underside, around the keyhole, were faint, recent scratches.

He let the lock hang, stood peering through the wire mesh. Dead still inside. A crow came swooping down overhead, cawing, and disappeared into the olive grove. Stillness again.

Call Joe Rinniak in Red Bluff? Not yet, not without some idea of what there was to find here.

Criminal trespass, like it or not.

Rinniak wouldn't care if it helped catch his firebug. Kelso might, but Kelso didn't have to know about it until later. A long time later, and word given to him by somebody else. Runyon didn't want anything more to do with the deputy if it could be avoided.

He fetched his flashlight and the Magnum in its carry holster. Clipped the holster to his belt, shoved the torch into a pants pocket to keep his hands free. Then he unhooked the padlock, eased himself through the opening, and closed the gates again behind him.

Out on the frontage road an approaching vehicle made a low-pitched rumbling noise. Sounded like a pickup truck, heading from the south in the direction of Gray's Landing. He stood still, waiting. The noise held steady as the truck passed by the compound; faded, and was gone.

The nearest of the buildings, the long shed, was off to his left. He went there first, fast-walking, the sun burning the back of his neck. Equipment and storage shed, probably. Two sets of doors, one on either end. The first set was locked. The second wasn't. One door half-creaked loudly when he pulled it open; the sound froze him again for a drag of seconds. He readied the flashlight in his left hand, wedged his body inside.

Thick gloom, stifling with trapped heat, rank with a mix of smells—oil, dust, heat, dry rot, rodent droppings. When he switched on the flashlight, the beam sent something small scurrying across the floor into darkness. One cavernous room, an area along one side that had once been a workshop, all of it empty now except for the car parked straight ahead of him at the back wall.

Dark blue '57 Impala with chrome rims, tuck-and-roll upholstery.

Both of its doors were locked. Runyon walked around it, shining the light inside through the windows. Empty.

He was running sweat when he stepped outside again. The heavy, breathless silence remained unbroken. He kept the flash in his left hand, his right on the butt of the Magnum, as he crossed to the shortish ell. A platform dock with two loading bays extended across two-thirds of the front. The one-third at the near end had once been the plant office. Two windows there, the panes all broken now, a couple starred with holes—probably the same sharpshooter who'd plinked the sign at the front entrance. Runyon poked the flash through one of the openings, switched it on. Debris, broken glass, an abandoned chair. Nobody had been here in a long time.

He climbed up onto the dock. Both metal doors secure. He found another door at the far end, this one a wooden single, and it was secure, too. Alongside it was a single window, the panes intact because they were protected from target practice by the back side of the warehouse building. A thick coating of grime wouldn't let the flashlight ray penetrate the glass. He tried the sash, but the latch was either locked down tight or frozen shut. Forget it. Nobody here, either.

Another dock with loading bays ran across the rear of

the warehouse building, the concrete cracked and chipped from age. Runyon crossed the yard, went up, and tried the metal doors there. Both locked tight. Down again, around to a single door set into the sidewall.

That was the one he was hunting for.

Shut but not secured. Opened inward a few inches as soon as he put pressure on it.

He stayed put for the better part of a minute, listening with his ear close to the opening. Silence inside. He drew his weapon, held it down along his side, and stepped into the gloomy interior.

A few thin rays of sunlight came through chinks in the outer walls, put a faint shine on the edges of the darkness. No other light. No sounds until he clicked on the flash—claws on wood somewhere nearby. He swung the beam in quick up-and-down arcs. Bottling room, judging from the long tables and left-behind jars and remains of a series of dismantled conveyor belts. Among the debris on the floor was a scatter of RipeOlive labels, some trod on and torn—the same kind as the fragment in his wallet. Dust lay thick and undisturbed except for a scuffed-up line of passage that led from the entrance door to an inner one in a partition wall straight ahead.

He followed the line, entered a second room. Faint brine smell in there, from the vats that lined it. Empty. The line bisected that room, too, extended through another doorway in a second partition wall.

Storage warehouse, twice the size of the previous two

spaces. Dead silence, the air so heat and dust choked it was difficult to breathe. He swept the light around. Broken pallets, broken crates, other rubble. Vertical support beams marking off sections. New smell he couldn't quite identify. He moved forward, widening the length and radius of the beam.

Halted its sweep, held it steady on what lay on the floor toward the far end.

Jerry Belsize.

Facedown, unmoving, arms outflung around one of the support beams, wrists bound together with a pair of handcuffs.

The kid was still alive—barely.

When Runyon knelt and touched him to feel for a pulse, his body jerked convulsively and then began to thrash, the arms pulling back until the cuffs clanked against the beam, the fingers hooking and spasming as if to fight off an attack. Runyon took his hand away. The thrashing stopped, but the spasming went on. The one eye turned his way didn't react to the light; it was open wide and seemed blind.

Belsize had been here a long time, left like this without food or water. Probably since sometime last Friday. His clothing, a pair of Levi's, Reeboks, a thin T-shirt, were torn and grimy. Face a mask of sweat-caked filth, lips cracked and swollen, a bloody wound on the right side of his head—the same kind of wound Runyon wore under the fresh bandage on his temple. Wrists and hands covered with dried blood, the skin ripped and abraded—the residue of frenzied struggles to free himself that had left the support beam splintered and deep-gouged from the chain links. Other marks were visible on the wrists and arms. Rodent bites. That was what he'd been trying to fight off in his delirium . . . rats, mice, attracted by the blood, making sharp-toothed forays in the dark.

Five days of nightmare.

Runyon had a strong stomach, but this type of cruelty was enough to sicken even the most case-hardened cop. Miracle that Belsize was still alive. Another day in here and he wouldn't have been. The only reason he'd survived this long was his youth and physical condition. As it was, he might not make it, and if he did, there was no telling what kind of mental shape he'd be in.

Runyon knew who was responsible. Knew it for sure now. Who, and some of the why.

He propped the torch so that the light was off the kid's face and steady on the handcuffed wrists. The arms and body were still quivering. Talked to him in a low, soft voice, telling him he was safe now, he'd soon be free, that he'd have to lie still so the handcuffs could be removed. He kept it up for several minutes, not sure if the words were having an effect until the quivering stopped and Belsize lay motionless once more. When he touched one wrist, it brought a spasm that lasted only a few seconds.

The cuffs were standard-issue. You could pick the locks

on them without too much strain if you knew what you were doing and had the right tools. Two minutes with the awl blade and corkscrew on his Swiss Army knife, talking the whole time to keep the kid still, and Runyon had one shackle open. Worry about the other one later. The steel circle had cut a deep blood-sealed furrow into the skin; he had to pry it loose. Gently he brought both stiffened arms out from around the beam, then turned Belsize onto his back. Brief struggle when he knelt to lift him. He waited until the struggles stopped, then got Belsize up off the floor and cradled against his body the way you'd hold a sick child. The way he might have held Joshua if he'd ever been given the chance.

He held the torch pressed between his fingers and the kid's body, the beam aimed downward to light the way through the building. But still he had to look straight down at his feet to see where he was going, avoid stumbling over something, and it was slow going. The dust clogged his sinuses; he was coughing, wheezing, by the time he reached the doorway at the far end, finally emerged into the bright dazzle of sunlight.

He was able to move a little more quickly then. Around the shed, across to the rear gates—pouring sweat, the muscles in his shoulders, arms, thighs, aching from the strain. At the Ford he lowered Belsize's feet, holding on to him with his right arm while he opened the rear door. Eased the kid inside, stretched him out on his back across the seat. His respiration was so slow Runyon had to check to make sure he was still breathing. He got the blanket he kept in the trunk, draped it over the inert form, arranged it so incoming sunlight wouldn't lie hot on Belsize's wounds. Before he slid in behind the wheel, he reset the padlock on the gates as he'd found it.

No question of calling 911 for an ambulance, waiting here until it arrived. Belsize could be dead by then. Make the hospital delivery himself, as fast as he could get to Red Bluff. And notify Rinniak on the way.

24

"Man, I hate this," Rinniak said. "I hate stakeouts."

Runyon stirred on the dark front seat of the county cruiser. Every time he shut himself down to make the waiting easier, Rinniak yanked him back. The man couldn't seem to sit still or keep still for more than a few minutes at a time.

"I never met anybody who didn't."

"Some are worse than others. Like this one."

"No argument there," Runyon said.

"I'm still having a hard time believing it. The scenario you laid out, I mean."

"You wouldn't be here if you didn't. Neither would I."

"I still hope you're wrong. Despite Jerry Belsize and the condition he's in."

"I'm not wrong."

"About tonight you could be."

Runyon said, "They keep getting bolder, taking more chances. Two days from the Silvera murder to the fire at the migrant camp. Two days from then until now. If not tonight, then tomorrow night."

"We can't risk another stakeout after this one. Word is bound to leak out about Belsize being alive, and if they get wind of it who knows what they'll do. We'll have to make the arrest tomorrow sometime and hope that Belsize doesn't die before he talks. What time is it now?"

"Almost eleven. If they're coming, it'll be pretty soon."

They'd been there since eight o'clock, pulled well back among the olive trees at the rear of the RipeOlive compound. A pair of Red Bluff deputies were in a second cruiser parked behind this one. The four of them had pulled brush up over the front ends to minimize the chance of headlight reflection off glass and metal, but if the firebugs did come, Runyon figured it would be with their lights off. A half-moon on the rise cast enough shine to drive by.

Both windows were down to let in a faint breeze that had kicked up an hour before. But the night was still hot, sultry, even at this hour. Crickets in the trees and dry grass made a singsong racket that rose and fell all around them. Through the windshield and down an avenue between shadowed tree trunks Runyon could see the rear gate and part of the chain-link fence on both sides. At an oblique angle, a section of the county blacktop to the north was also visible.

Rinniak said, "Games, for Christ's sake. As if arson and murder and false imprisonment weren't enough."

"It's all wrapped up together."

"Yeah. I should have tumbled to it myself, some of it anyway, but it got by me. I just didn't see any of it."

"Too close to the situation."

"That's no excuse." Rinniak shifted position, blew out his breath in a hissing sigh. "Sick thrills. People nowadays . . . so damn jaded."

"That's part of it. See how far they can push the envelope."

"Devil's work. You suppose that's why they killed Silvera?"

"I don't know. Maybe. It's not the reason they intended to kill Jerry Belsize."

"Retribution. Revenge."

"It's the only explanation that makes sense."

"What the hell could he have done to them?"

"I made you a guess earlier."

"That's not enough to torture him like that, kill him."

"It might be to them."

"So goddamn normal on the outside, and on the inside, lunatics out of control . . . Christ, I just can't seem to get my head around it. Nothing like this ever happened in this county before."

"And probably won't again."

"Take a long time for people to get over it," Rinniak said grimly. "And some of them never will."

They lapsed into silence again. That suited Runyon. He'd been over it and over it with Rinniak and the sheriff, Macon, after he left the hospital and then again on the drive down here and during the long wait since. Rinniak couldn't seem to let go of the concept. Just kept picking at it verbally, often enough to indicate that he was doing the same inside his head. Runyon didn't blame him. He'd done enough thinking about it himself. Too much. He tried to turn himself off again, didn't have as much success this time.

Eleven fifteen by the luminous dial of his watch.

The night breeze sharpened, then just as suddenly died. The cricket sound seemed to grow steadily louder, as if it were building toward some kind of crescendo.

Eleven thirty.

Eleven forty.

Rinniak said, "Headlights coming," as he had each of the other few times a set had appeared from the direction of Gray's Landing.

"I see them."

The beams threw a sheen of brightness on the dark sky, made silhouette shapes of the RipeOlive buildings as they drew closer. The previous headlights had been hidden as the vehicles passed by, then reappeared briefly on the far side before they vanished. Not these. The car slowed as it came past the water tower, made a quick, sharp turn onto the plant road. As soon as it bounced up over the railroad right-of-way, the headlamps went dark.

"By God, Runyon, you were right. It's them."

"Looks like it."

They watched the car swing over onto the dirt road, raise dust as it followed the fence line around. Pale moonlight put a sleek gleam on its metal surfaces. It rolled along slow to the rear gates, stopped close to it on the near side; the engine noise died. Nothing happened for a time, long enough to cause Rinniak to say, "What the hell are they waiting for?" Then both doors opened at once and the two of them got out. Both wore dark clothing, dark caps of some kind. One opened the trunk, handed out a pair of rectangular objects that had to be gallon tins of kerosene. The other things that came out were small, unidentifiable blobs. Timing device and flashlights, probably.

The shorter one carrying both tins, they went to the gate and inside at an angle to the far corner of the shed. Blended into the deep shadows cast by the building.

Rinniak was already out of the cruiser by then. Runyon and the two deputies joined him. Nobody said anything; they'd already worked out the logistics. Single file, each with a six-cell torch, the four of them picked their way out of the grove, across the road, and through the open gate. The deputies took up positions along the near side of the shed. Runyon followed Rinniak to the far end, into the heavy darkness along the sidewall. You couldn't see the unlocked warehouse door from the front corner, but it wouldn't matter unless the firebugs went the other way when they came out, and it didn't figure they would.

It wasn't a long wait. Voices drifted out of the shadows first, one louder than the other, angry. Shapes, then, the leader moving fast across the moonlit yard, the other one lugging the kerosene tins. Still talking to each other, the words distinguishable now.

". . . how he could've gotten free."

"Pulled the handcuffs loose somehow, damn him."

"Oh God, he'll tell on us. What if he already has?"

"Don't get excited. He couldn't've been gone long. Or got far after five days in there."

"You think he might still be around here somewhere?"

"Dead, I hope. We'll look before we set the timer."

"We're not going ahead with the fire . . . ?"

"Like hell we're not."

Rinniak murmured, "Like hell you are," and touched Runyon's arm, and they stepped out together and put the lights on.

"County sheriff's officers. Stand where you are."

The stabbing glare brought them up short; the command rooted them in place. Sandra Parnell dropped both kerosene tins, one arm lifting to shield her eyes; she stood in a terrified freeze, like a jacklit deer. Ashley Kelso's bug-eyed stare held a mix of fury and disbelief.

The two deputies came pounding up, their lights joining the others. "Kelso's daughter, all right," one of them said. Another one having trouble coming to terms with it.

Rinniak started forward, saying, "You're under arrest—"

The rest of it got lost in a sudden shrieked "No!" from the Kelso girl. She threw her flashlight at Rinniak, missing him, and bolted—a stumbling headlong charge toward the back fence.

Runyon was closest to her flight path. He cut her off, chased her down, managed to catch hold of her arm. She rounded on him, cursing, spitting like a cat, and clawed stinging furrows into the back of his hand, tried to get at his face with those flashing nails, tried to kick him in the groin. He threw the six-cell down and fastened grips on both arms, jerked her around, and bent her back hard against an upthrust knee. She kept on fighting him, screaming obscenities. One of the deputies was there by then and she fought him, too, tried to bite him. It took both men to wrestle her to the ground, Runyon to hold her down while the deputy shackled her hands behind her back.

The fight went out of her. But not the viciousness. She rolled over, sat up glaring at Runyon. "You!" she said. "You son of a bitch, *you* did this!"

He ignored her. Blood ran from the scratches on his hand, trickling between the fingers. He wrapped his handkerchief around it.

"I should've killed you in the barn!" Ashley screamed. "I should've hung you up with Manny like I wanted to!"

The deputy said, "You better be quiet, kid—"

"Fuck you!"

He took her arm, roughly, and lifted her to her feet.

"Leave me alone!" She looked at Runyon again. "Jerry's dead, isn't he? Tell me he's dead."

"He's not."

"You're lying."

"He's in the hospital in Red Bluff. Expected to live."

"Shit!" She squinted past him, to where the other deputy was putting handcuffs on Sandra Parnell while Rinniak recited her rights. "Where is he? Why isn't he here?"

Ashley wasn't asking about Jerry Belsize now. Runyon knew who she meant, but the deputy said, "You heard him. In the hospital."

"Not him, my father. Don Kelso, the big tough cop. Didn't anybody tell him? I wish he could see me right now. Pay *him* back, the son of a bitch. No more telling me what to do, what not to do, how to live my life. No more orders, no more bullshit, no more Daddy's good little girl!"

"Jesus," the deputy said.

Sandra Parnell began to cry.

Rinniak finished helping the deputies load the two women into the caged backseat of their cruiser, came over to where Runyon stood waiting. "Okay," he said wearily. "How's your hand?"

"It'll be all right."

"You should have it looked at."

"A little iodine's all it needs. I've had enough of doctors and hospitals."

They got into Rinniak's car. Before he started the engine he said, "I keep thinking I should've let Kelso know before we came here. I've worked with the man off and on for ten years, I owed him that much."

"He wouldn't have gone along with this."

"No. He wouldn't."

"Even if he had, you heard what she said. Twice as bad for him if he'd been here."

"You're right. Spared him that much, at least. But he's got to know now and it's my job to tell him. And it should be in person."

"You can drop me off somewhere first."

"I said should be in person. Truth is, I don't think I can face him right now. So I'll do it the coward's way and call him from Red Bluff." Rinniak put the cruiser in gear, eased it forward. "I have kids of my own," he said. "One of my daughters is about Ashley's age."

"So's my son."

"Then you know why I can't face Kelso right now."

"Yes," Runyon said, "I know why."

25

I spent that night going over facts and suppositions, by myself and with Tamara and Kerry. Tamara had dug up two more pieces of connected, corroborating, circumstantial evidence—all there was left to find. On Wednesday morning I went to see Irv Blaustein at Pacific Rim Insurance and had a long talk with him.

Same conclusion, down the line.

There was nothing to do then but make an appointment with Celeste Ogden and deliver the news to her.

I f anyone killed your sister, Mrs. Ogden, it was Anthony Drax."

No visible reaction. She sat on the tufted velvet couch in her living room, her back straight, her hands palms up in the lap of her black slacks—the same posture as on my previous visit and in Dr. Prince's office yesterday. Same expressionless demeanor, too.

"If?" she said.

"He was there the night she died and his actions indicate a certain amount of guilt, but whether he was directly responsible is open to question. If he was, it probably wasn't a premeditated act."

"Of course it was premeditated. On *his* orders."

"If a crime was committed, it's not likely Mathias was complicit except as a catalyst."

"You're not making sense. Why do you keep saying 'if'?"

On the table in front of her was the file printout Tamara and I had put together, but Mrs. Ogden hadn't opened the envelope. She wanted a verbal report first, which made this even more difficult for me.

I said, "It's also possible your sister's death was just what it was ruled to be, an accident."

"I don't believe that for a second."

"I'm sorry, but the facts support more than one theory."

"Will you please get to the point? Tell me why you believe Drax is guilty."

She wasn't going to let me ease into explanations. All right then. Facts. I told her about the Mathiases' neighbor Mary Conti and what she'd seen at approximately ten o'clock on the night Nancy Mathias died. I gave her the information Tamara had turned up: the three-year-old BMW Z3 owned by Drax's girlfriend, Donna Lane, was silver colored; she'd been working a flight to Dallas on the night of the murder; the car registered to Drax had been in the shop for repairs on that same date.

"There's one more thing that points to him," I said

then. The main thing, thanks to Kerry's sharp eye. "The last entry in your sister's diary."

". . . You mean the question 'why adhere'?"

"Yes. Only it's not the question we all took it to be. She wasn't asking herself why she should stay in the marriage."

"What, then?"

"Let me give you the reasoning first. Your sister often worked in her study at night, paying bills, writing in her diary. We know that from the date-and-time lines on the diary entries. And from the fact that Mrs. Conti often saw lights on in the upstairs front room. That is where Nancy's study was?"

"Yes."

"Directly above the front entrance."

"Yes."

"Was her desk close to the windows?"

"Close to them, yes."

"Her last diary entry was made at ten-oh-five P.M. That's approximately the same time Mrs. Conti saw the stranger park his car, walk toward Nancy's house, and vanish. Suppose your sister had just opened up the diary file to make a new entry when the doorbell interrupted her. Suppose she swung around to the windows, looked out and down. Mrs. Conti said the night-light over the front door was on. Would Nancy have been able to see who was ringing the bell at that late hour?"

"Yes, if he was standing back slightly from the door. It's set flush in the wall; there's no vestibule."

"Then suppose she was surprised and puzzled enough

at the visitor's identity to turn back to the computer and type that last sentence before she went downstairs to answer the bell. If it was on and open to the diary file, it's not unlikely she'd have done something like that under the circumstances."

"No. It's not."

"But it was an impulsive act and she was in a hurry, distracted. The question she was asking was the one in her mind at the moment, and when she typed it out she used her usual brand of shorthand—but she also made a pair of typing errors that she either didn't notice or didn't bother to correct, and that changed the entire meaning of the sentence. She touched the Caps Lock key when she shifted to type the first letter, so that the rest of the question was in capital letters. Three words, not two. Or rather, two words and one set of initials. Her second mistake was not hitting the space bar to separate the initials from the last word. The question wasn't 'Why adhere?'; it was 'Why AD here?' AD—Anthony Drax."

Celeste Ogden nodded stiffly. "But you don't think he went there with the intention of killing her."

"No, I don't," I said. "Drax is a smart man, and smart men don't plan crimes where there's a strong risk of being seen in the neighborhood, as he was seen. It's more likely he went there to talk to her. If he did kill her, it was probably the result of tempers flaring out of control—a shove, an unintentional blow, a fall that resulted in a fatal head trauma. That kind of thing happens all too often."

"Nancy wouldn't have invited him upstairs. Or are you saying he didn't push her down the stairs?"

"Not the way you mean. In that scenario he panicked when he saw she was dead and tried to cover up by making it look like an accident. Carried her upstairs and threw the body down. Found her key and locked the door after him when he left. The other possible scenario is that he did nothing except argue with her and then leave. She was upset; she went upstairs; she tripped or lost her balance and fell."

"Is that what you think happened?"

"There's just no way of knowing. Two things argue for the first scenario—the length of time Drax was in the house, more than half an hour, if Mrs. Conti's memory is accurate, and the fact that he was hurrying, staying in the shadows, coat collar pulled up, when she saw him the second time, as if he was anxious to get away from there. But both could also have innocent explanations."

Celeste Ogden got up and paced over to the windows, stood looking out at the city. It was quiet in the big sunroom, quiet in the penthouse flat. Somewhere I could hear a clock ticking, the only discernible sound. We were alone in the penthouse; Mrs. Ogden had let me in herself this time.

With her back to me she said, "Why would Drax want to talk to Nancy at that time of night?"

"It's the kind of thing a man like him would do if he knew she was dying, knew she was angry at her husband

and threatening divorce. Try to convince her to change her mind, stay with Mathias and keep quiet about her condition for his sake."

That brought her around. "Now what are you saying? That Nancy was killed because she had a brain tumor?"

"Directly or indirectly, yes."

"That's insane!"

"I agree. But it's the only reasonable explanation."

"Why? *Why?* She would have been dead in six months."

God, I hated this. I tried not to squirm as Celeste Ogden came back and sat down again. "Or she might have lived a year or more," I said. "A long, difficult year for her and her husband—doctor and hospital visits, time demands, gradual physical deterioration, all the rest of it. The kind of situation you can't ignore, can't control, can't keep under wraps."

"Him," she said as if she were uttering an obscenity.

"What I think happened," I said slowly and carefully, "is that Mathias confided the situation to Drax. Needed to vent to somebody with the same mind-set who would understand his point of view. That's what I meant about him being a catalyst. Nancy was forcing him to stand by her with the threat of divorce, of going public with her illness and what a coldhearted bastard he is—creating a scandal that might potentially damage his image, the IPO, his long-range plans. Yet if he played the dutiful husband it would mean putting his business interests on partial hold, delegating responsibility to underlings like Drax, and that could also be damaging. He was between a rock and a hard place."

"Sufficient motive for paying Drax to commit murder."

"Yes, but I don't think he did. Even if the idea occurred to him, he's too cautious, too self-protective, to take such a huge risk. I think it was Drax's own idea to see Nancy that night. Mathias may or may not know about it; if he does, it's in his best interest to keep quiet about it, and about Nancy's terminal diagnosis, and let her death stand as an accident. Same for Drax, guilty or innocent. Nobody else besides Dr. Prince, as far as they're aware, knows about the brain tumor; it didn't turn up in the routine autopsy because the medical examiner wasn't looking for it."

"Savages, both of them," Celeste Ogden said. "Monsters."

I didn't dispute it.

Almost immediately she was on her feet again. Yesterday she'd been calm and stationary throughout the explanation of her sister's malignancy; today she couldn't seem to sit still, as if the latest shock had unleashed something inside her. I watched her walk around the room picking up decorative knickknacks and putting them down again, straightening and rearranging paintings and wall hangings that didn't need straightening or rearranging. That went on for three or four minutes. Then, abruptly, she sat down again in the same rigid, palms-up posture as before. Nothing had changed on the blank screen of her face, not even when she referred to Drax and Mathias as monsters.

"All right," she said. "Do you call the police or shall I?"

"Neither of us."

"What?"

"We can't go to the police. It wouldn't do any good."

"What are you talking about?"

This was the worst part, the part I'd been dreading most. Bite the bullet; get it said.

"There's no case against Drax, not even a circumstantial one. It's all ifs and maybes, supposition and guesswork. No witnesses except for Mrs. Conti, and it was too dark for her to identify the man she saw. No crime-scene evidence. No evidence that Drax was in the neighborhood or inside the house that night. No probable cause for the police to arrest and charge him, much less for the district attorney to prosecute him."

She stared at me. "Confront him, make him confess."

"He'd only deny it and keep denying it. So would Mathias. Men like them never willingly incriminate themselves."

"Beat it out of him then."

"I don't operate that way, Mrs. Ogden. And it wouldn't do any good if I did. Confessions made under duress won't stand up in a court of law. He'd recant it, have me thrown in jail, hire a lawyer, and sue me out of business."

On her feet. Down again. "His fingerprints . . . they must still be in the house."

"Probably, unless Mathias has had the place cleaned since. But they don't prove anything. Fingerprints can't be dated and Drax was a visitor there before."

"Then for God's sake find some other kind of proof. That's what I hired you for."

"I can't do that, either."

"Why can't you? I'll pay you whatever you ask—"

"It isn't a question of money. Or time. Or effort. The damn lousy fact is, there's no proof to find. It doesn't exist any longer, if it ever did. It stopped existing when Drax drove away that night and the Palo Alto police ruled Nancy's death accidental and closed the case."

The emotionless facade broke down all at once. It was like watching a wall collapse. Rage, disbelief, frustration, all ran dark and hot in her eyes and in her voice when she said, "Damn you, what are you telling me? Are you telling me nothing can be done, *nothing*? They're going to get away with it, both of them?"

What could I say? That things always work out neatly in the end and life always delivers easy answers to difficult problems? That there's no such thing as a perfect crime? That one way or another the guilty are always punished, justice is always done? No, I couldn't lie to her. Some loose ends don't get tied off, some problems don't get solved, perfect crimes happen more often than you can imagine, the guilty all too often go free, there's more than one reason the statue of Justice is blind. That's the way things are. You have to accept it and deal with it.

But all I could manage was, "I'm sorry, Mrs. Ogden."

"No. No! I won't stand for it."

"I'm afraid you don't have any choice."

"There's always a choice. Another detective . . . a criminal attorney . . ."

"That's your prerogative. But give them the facts as I've given them to you, and they'll tell you the same thing. There's nothing they can do. There's nothing anybody can do."

Up again. "Get out of here," she said. "I don't want anything more to do with you. Get out of my sight."

I didn't blame her for that. She had nobody else to take it out on; might as well be me.

I beat it out of there without another word.

26

JAKE RUNYON

It was late Wednesday afternoon before he finally got on the highway back to San Francisco. Tamara understood about the delay when he called her to explain, but he still didn't like leaving her and Bill hanging an extra day, unavoidable or not. He'd been away too long already.

One reason was the long night; he didn't get to bed until almost 3:00 A.M. Another was that he had to go back to the sheriff's department in Red Bluff to sign a written statement of what he'd told Rinniak and Sheriff Macon the day before.

Rinniak was there, bleak and haggard, when Runyon arrived late in the morning, and they had a few minutes together. The two women had made separate signed confessions by then, Sandra Parnell tearfully, Ashley Kelso gloatingly. Turned out they were lovers, bisexuals—one angle he hadn't figured on. No real surprises in the rest of it. Rinniak made no mention of Kelso, and Runyon didn't ask.

Ashley was the leader, of course. Paranoid schizophrenic with a persecution complex—you didn't need to be Freud to see that. She hated her father because of his strict authoritarian ways and she hated Jerry Belsize because she'd given him her virginity and he wouldn't stand up to Kelso or have anything more to do with her after the ass-kicking incident. She itched to pay back both of them for the imagined hurt they'd done to her and, in her words, "have fun doing it." Some of the "fun" had been spur-of-the-moment, but most had been planned over a period of months.

She and Sandra were still friends even though she had taken Ashley's place with Belsize; the Parnell girl looked up to her. Ashley took their relationship to a different level by seducing her, "making her fall in love with me." That gave her a hold on the weaker woman that became controlling, hypnotic. Sandra would do anything Ashley said—the torching of empty and abandoned places, for starters, using tins of kerosene Ashley swiped from Battle Hardware. Since she was a kid, Ashley had been "getting off on watching things burn," the sexual thrill common to most firebugs. She also saw to it that Jerry found out about the homosexual affair—the reason he'd broken up with Sandra, told his parents that she wasn't the girl he'd thought she was, and didn't want anything more to do with her. Their relationship was stagnant anyway because of her deepening involvement with Ashley.

The breakup allowed Ashley to turn Sandra against Jerry, convince her that he deserved payback, manipulate her into the kidnap scheme. They lured him out to RipeOlive with the promise of three-way sex, and he was just dumb enough to go along with it. Ashley clobbered him with her favorite weapon; they dragged him into the warehouse and used a pair of her father's handcuffs to leave him shackled to the beam. She didn't care if he was alive or dead when they went back last night to torch the buildings. All she wanted, she said, was to watch him burn.

The murder of Manuel Silvera had been premeditated. He'd seen Ashley and Sandra leaving the scene of the barn fire, made the mistake of going to Ashley about it instead of her father. Like a lot of people in Gray's Landing, Silvera was afraid of Kelso, but he was a moral man and his conscience wouldn't let him keep quiet about what he'd seen. Ashley saw killing him as the perfect way to shut his mouth and blame Jerry at the same time. There was another reason, too: she was curious to know what it felt like to kill somebody. She arranged to meet Silvera in the barn Friday night, made the anonymous call to the Belsizes to lure them away, hit him with the two-by-two when he wasn't looking. Stringing him up was what she called "an inspiration"; she'd never seen anybody hanged before, and the idea excited her. After she and Sandra finished planting the false evidence in the hayloft and in Jerry's room, they went back to the barn for one more look at their handiwork—and that was when Runyon arrived.

They hid behind the stack of lumber, and he got the same two-by-two treatment as Silvera. He might've gotten the hanging treatment, too, if the Belsizes hadn't come back when they did.

The game playing was partly kicks, partly a means of tightening the frame around Jerry, partly payback against Runyon; Ashley was pissed at him for showing up at the farm and almost spoiling her plans. Jerry had never been in the trailer at the migrant workers' camp. The whole thing—roach butts, sleeping bag, fast-food remains, Sandra coming to Runyon with her plea for help, the anonymous phone call to Kelso—was an elaborate setup. Sandra hadn't wanted to do it—she was afraid of Runyon as well as Kelso—but Ashley forced her into it. She hadn't been told in advance about the anonymous call; her reaction to Kelso's arrival on Sunday had been genuine. Ashley's little surprise joke.

Runyon had figured out the sham even before he found Belsize, been pretty sure then that Ashley and Sandra were the real perps. Too many inconsistencies, too many lies. Jerry didn't drive like a maniac or run down dogs in the road or beat up on his women—that was game playing and character assassination. He didn't do drugs, had never bought weed from Gus Mayerhof. But Ashley did and had. Nobody knew Jerry or had seen him in Lost Bar because he'd never been there. Sandra hadn't seen him on Friday night because he was already shackled at RipeOlive by then, and Jerry's father hadn't told her that Runyon was a detective because she hadn't talked to his parents in weeks. The little scene between Ashley and Sandra in the restaurant parking lot on Saturday night had been staged, too. Ashley made a slip then that Runyon hadn't caught until later. "I'll bet if Jerry hit you any harder with that two-by-two, he'd've taken your head right off." Unlikely that either her father or Rinniak would have told her the exact nature of the weapon. There was only one other way she could've known.

The label fragment hadn't gotten into the trailer on the bottom of Jerry's shoe but on the bottom of Ashley's or Sandra's. Once Mayor Battle had identified it, Runyon remembered Jerry's summer job at RipeOlive a few years ago and Rinniak telling him Sandra's father had worked for the olive processors. The fact that Martin Parnell headed the skeleton crew before RipeOlive shut down for good made it a fair bet he'd had keys and still had them. Simple enough for Sandra to lift the ones to the rear gate and the warehouse door and return them later.

All of this Runyon had told Rinniak and Macon yesterday after he delivered Jerry Belsize to the hospital ER. And it was all in the statement he signed.

On the way out of the station he saw Kelso coming in. Dressed as usual in full uniform down to the Sam Browne belt and holstered revolver. Same cowboy walk, same aggressive jaw thrust, everything in place and untouched. Except for the eyes. The eyes were as dead as a corpse's. One glance passed between them; Kelso's went right through him. Best that way. Even if he'd been on friendly terms with the man, Runyon would have had nothing to say to him. His only child hated him, too, with a deep and abiding hatred, but they didn't even have that in common.

Joshua, despite his problems, was a responsible member of society.

Ashley was a demon seed.

The third reason he didn't get on the road until late was Jerry Belsize. Rinniak had told him the kid's condition was critical, but that he was conscious and responding to medical treatment and would probably pull through. On Runyon's first trip to the hospital, a few minutes past noon, a nurse told him visitors would probably be permitted for a short period, but that it wouldn't be until after a doctor's examination at two o'clock. So he was forced to waste two hours with lunch and some aimless driving around Red Bluff.

Belsize's parents were there when Runyon was admitted to the ward room at two thirty, and he had to endure a weepy round of gratitude from them. The kid was doped up and foggy and didn't seem to be tracking too well; he didn't have much to say other than a whispered thanks. Runyon didn't stay long. He wouldn't have stayed long in any case.

Before he left he did what he had to do, even though it cost him some of the parental goodwill and made him feel like a shit.

He served Gerald Belsize with his subpoena.

27

Folie à deux," Kerry said.

"Come again?"

"It's a psychiatric syndrome, also known as shared psychotic disorder or induced delusional disorder. Where a paranoid delusional system develops in one person as a result of a close relationship with another who has or is capable of a similar delusional system. Literal translation: madness shared by two."

"I've heard of it. And?"

"Well, I've been thinking. From what you told me about the firebug case Jake was involved in up north, I'll bet that's what was operating there—folie à deux. Strong, domineering woman infects a weaker, less intelligent friend and lover with her insanity and together they commit public outrages—arson, murder, false imprisonment, torture. Contributing factors of sexual perversion, if you can call it that, and religion and rebellion against parental authority.

It's not exactly a classic case, but it does have a lot of the elements."

"If you say so. What's your point?"

"My point," she said, "is that in a way you were dealing with a case of folie à deux at the same time—you and Tamara and I. How's that for a crazy coincidence?"

It was early Thursday afternoon and we'd just finished having lunch at the Gold Mirror, her favorite neighborhood Italian restaurant. She was on her second glass of red wine, which always makes her a little flakey and unpredictable.

"What case?"

"The Mathias case, of course."

"I don't want to talk about the Mathias case."

"Just let me tell you my theory and we'll drop the subject."

"All right. How do you figure it's another folie à deux?"

"Well, it's obvious when you think about it. A brilliant sociopath, Mathias, cares so little about his dying wife that he wishes her dead sooner so she won't interfere with his business plans, and communicates this to another sociopath with a similar bent and an inferior intellect, Drax, who acts on it."

"Not intentionally and not on direct order."

"Doesn't matter. Drax was infected just the same."

"The two of them may be sick, but they're not delusional."

"They are if they think they're normal."

"No religious or sexual motivation or rebellion," I said.

"You could make a case that hero worship is a form of latent sexuality."

"Now you're really reaching."

"Anyhow, Drax wouldn't have gone to see Nancy Mathias that night if he wasn't infected to some degree with his boss's psychosis. Wouldn't have killed her, accidentally or otherwise. Subconsciously he was carrying out Mathias's wishes, and he covered up the crime to protect Mathias as well as himself."

"My wife, the wannabe shrink."

"Be scornful if you want, but I like my theory. Parallel cases of folie à deux."

"With opposite resolutions."

"I know, but that doesn't change the psychological implications."

No point in arguing with her after two glasses of red wine. Pretty soon I said, "You know, you can make anything fit any concept if you try hard enough."

"I suppose that's true."

"Folie à deux, for instance. You could say we suffer from a form of it ourselves. We have a close relationship and I'm crazy in love with you and my madness has infected you and made you crazy in love with me. A couple of delusional nutcases."

"Delusional?"

"Okay, just plain nuts."

"I won't argue that. So which of us is dominant and which the weaker intellect?"

"Sometimes it's me; sometimes it's you. We're democratic nutcases."

"You have a point," she said. "There's plenty of sexual motivation, too. Even what some bluenose types might consider perversion, now and then."

"Let's not get started on that topic again."

"Why not? It's on both our minds."

"Premature, that's why."

"Only by a week or so. Besides, I can't help it if I'm caught in the clutches of the mania you infected me with."

"I'm still not sure we ought to rush back into things."

"We're not rushing; we're easing into it. Kind of like foreplay."

"Kerry . . ."

"Oh, don't be stuffy. It's my decision to make, or don't you think so?"

"Not if you're hurt by it."

"I've been hurt by a lot worse and you know it. The decision is mine in any case." She smiled suddenly. "My folly à do or folly à don't, you might say."

"Huh?"

"Never mind. You just leave everything to me. It won't be spur-of-the-moment, either. I'll give you plenty of advance warning."

"What for?"

"So we can arrange for Emily to sleep over at a friend's."

"Why is that necessary?"

"If we're alone," Kerry said, "think of all the noise we can make."

28

Some things, like Kerry's breast cancer, do work out pretty much as you want them to. Other things take a sudden bizarre twist and tie off loose ends in ways that you didn't see coming at all.

I'd told Celeste Ogden that there was nothing she or anybody else could do to prevent Anthony Drax from getting away with the murder of her sister, or Brandon Mathias from getting away with his tacit role in the crime. But she proved me wrong. Dead wrong.

Nine days after our last meeting, she waited in the RingTech parking lot for the two men to come out together and emptied her husband's 9 mm Beretta into their bodies—seven rounds at point-blank range. Drax died at the scene. Mathias died six hours later at a Palo Alto hospital.

She did it for Nancy, she told police calmly and matter-of-factly. She couldn't bear the thought of them going unpunished; they were evil, pitiless men who did not deserve to live. Nancy would not be able to rest in peace as long as they were alive, and neither would she. She'd spent three sleepless nights thinking about it, summoning her courage. And then she'd destroyed them.

And destroyed herself at the same time.

And left me feeling partially responsible, an unwitting catalyst in my own right, when I heard the news.

Justice?

You tell me.